MW01236289

ONE

a novel

by
Catherine Farnes

PRESS

ONE
by Catherine Farnes

Printed in the United States of America

ISBN 1-59781-200-5

www.xulonpress.com

For John,
Ian, Caitlyn, Bethany, and Nathan

With Thanks To:

Pastor Thad Arnold
Pastor Mike Backhaus
Pastor Dave Johnson
Lisa Kilsdonk
Pastor Ben Lahay
Pastors Ron and LaVonne Masters
Pastor Keith Stone

What did Jesus mean when He prayed in John 17 that His followers would be ONE even as He and the Father are ONE?
Are we as Christians, His Church as a whole, getting the job done?
Are we even coming close?

1

Six teenagers, four boys and two girls, crept across an empty parking lot toward a modern church building. The leader could feel the five behind him. Following him in every way. Their actions. Their minds. Their passion.

The town's business district lay dark between mostly untraveled streets at this time of night. But the teenagers walked quietly, not even wanting the soles of their shoes on the pavement to make noise, though they'd be making plenty of noise in just a few minutes.

With only the pale blue glow from the lighted cross atop the church and the reflection of the city lights on the clouds to guide them, and so much huge darkness to hide them, they ran to the church's front doors and hid for a moment in the shadows there, making sure they hadn't been noticed.

They hadn't.

With a whispered "Let's do it!" from the leader, they began.

Three of them painted.

Two of them smashed windows and busted down the sign on the lawn that announced service times in small white letters and the pastor's name in larger ones.

When they finished, the leader emptied a paper bag full of newspaper clippings onto the glass covered floor just inside the front doors.

Then they left. Faster than they had come. Their spray cans, bats, and laughter no longer concealed.

Nobody heard or saw them.

But in the morning, Sunday, everyone would see what they had done.

"Wait," the leader said, suddenly thinking of something else. While the other five teenagers waited in the trees along the edge of the parking lot, he ran back toward the building. The *church*. He could smell the weeds. The still wet paint. His own sweat.

Once at the front door again, he reached his gloved hand carelessly through the shattered glass and felt along the wall for the switch he was certain to find there. When his fingers touched it, he pushed down the only lever that was up.

The lighted cross above him flickered and buzzed before going black and silent.

Punctuation for his statement.

* * *

Corey Gress was not a jumpy camper. He slept all night at home without every sound tearing him out of sleep and that's the way he slept in his tent. Usually.

He rolled onto his side and pulled his knees up as far as his sleeping bag would permit, stubbornly refusing to open his eyes. A bear could be in camp and he wouldn't care. As long as it stayed out of, off of, and away from his tent. His handgun lay in easy reach at his side. If a nose poked at the side of the tent, a growl, that unmistakable odor of griz, then he'd think about maybe getting out of his bag. Barring that, though, he'd just as soon stay warm, thanks. And asleep.

Anyway, there was no bear in camp tonight.

Corey had grown up in these mountains. Back - packing, camping, fishing, snowmobiling, shooting, rock climbing. And since his sixteenth birthday two years ago, he'd come frequently without his father. He was used to the sounds of the wilderness at night. The whine of the wind in dry branches and between the sides of the tent and the rainfly. Coyotes. The snappings and sizzlings of the dying fire. The rustle of his sleeping bag whenever he moved. But all of these sounds, with the help of a prejudiced and frightened imagination, had so far robbed his friend Justin of any sleep.

This was the city kid's first time camping and it showed. While hurrying out of the tent a moment ago, probably to go water a nearby tree, Justin had neglected to put on his boots, grab a flashlight, or rezip the tent door. So Corey listened for him.

Though Corey had many friends and always had, Justin, who had moved west from New York only six months earlier, was probably his closest. Justin was two years younger, but the two understood each other. And Corey enjoyed helping Justin settle into the slower pace of life in western Montana.

Unfortunately, Justin didn't appear to be enjoying the rugged camping thing as much as Corey had hoped he would.

"Justin?" he called out, poking his face halfway out of his sleeping bag. "You okay?"

No answer.

He called again. Louder.

Still no answer.

This concerned Corey. Alarmed him. It didn't take this long to rid yourself of that last mug of hot chocolate, especially when it was 35 degrees outside and you were scared to death besides.

"Justin?"

Justin's mother had not agreed easily to the idea of her son backpacking in the *wilduhniss* where there could be *beahs* and *crazy hermit types* behind every tree, but Corey had assured her that he knew how to handle any situation that might conceivably come up.

And that's exactly what he intended to do. Handle the situation.

He pulled on his boots, clicked on his flashlight and stepped out of the tent.

* * *

Nearly midnight. Will Cooper slid forward on his chair, knowing he should have been home two hours ago but not wanting to leave just yet. In the past whenever Jon Hale had invited him to this church-type but not church Christian coffeehouse, Will had always found reasons to stay home. He had no room in his thinking for Jon's ideas about God. For *any* ideas about God. He was sixteen years old and had so far seen very little if any evidence of a supposedly omnipotent being in his world. But tonight, when he'd had nowhere else to go and had to get away from his angry drunk father, he'd decided he might as well give it a try. If nothing else maybe he'd get a good laugh or two. Who couldn't use a good laugh or two?

But Will Cooper wasn't laughing.

Could there really be a God who cared about him? A God who would love him the way his father never had? A God who had made a way for Will to know Him, even after all the weak, wrong, and stupid things Will had said, thought, and done?

Jon Hale and his friends said *yes*. Absolutely.

Will tried to imagine how it would be to believe that. To really believe that.

He couldn't.

Will could not reconcile—though he found himself longing to do exactly that—the concept of a God, loving or otherwise, but especially loving, with what had happened in his family. Will didn't remember his mother. She had died when he was only three. Some kind of car accident. His father had destroyed all her pictures and deliberately kept Will out of contact with any of her family. Remembering was too hard on him, he'd told Will.

But Will knew his father hadn't stopped remembering.

Remembering and drinking. Hating life. Hating Will.

Will's stomach began to hurt so he pushed his chair away from the table and stood to leave. Coming to the coffeehouse had been a mistake. A big one. Even his father's fist in his face would feel better than his own foolish wanting to believe in a God that couldn't be true or real. Or worse, *was* real and had allowed his mother's life to be taken and his father's to be turned into a drunken waste, robbing Will of both of his parents.

Quickly, almost rudely, he said goodbye to Jon Hale and hurried outside to his pickup.

"Will? Wait a second."

Great. Jon had followed him. The mid-July breeze was cooler than it had been before sunset but still felt warm and dry against his face. Will thought about not stopping, pretending he hadn't heard Jon, but decided to wait. Jon was a good friend. Will's only good friend.

"Are you all right, Will?"

"I gotta get home, is all."

Jon stared at him for several seconds, clearly perceiving that Will wasn't being totally honest, but willing to leave it alone. Will always appreciated that about Jon. The way he never tried to force Will to talk. The way he stayed content with knowing that Will knew he could talk to him if he wanted to.

Sometimes Will did want to talk to Jon Hale. But tonight wasn't one of those times. "See you later," he said, climbing into his truck. "I gotta get home." As he drove away, leaving Jon standing alone in the parking lot, he glanced at his watch. Ten past twelve.

Please, he prayed to the God he didn't believe in, *please let my father be passed out on the couch when I get home.*

I'm late.

* * *

Justin heard Corey push the tent flap open and saw his light as he made his way outside. He wanted to yell to him to get back in. To not move. But he couldn't. He couldn't even breathe.

"Justin?"

The flashlight beam moved back and forth ahead of Corey as he approached the smoldering fire… Justin…the *thing* on the rock behind him.

When the light shone on Justin, standing less than fifteen feet from the tent, Corey said, "What's the problem, Jus—?" Then he stopped.

He had seen the problem.

And the problem didn't appreciate light in its eyes.

* * *

After getting off work at the restaurant at quarter past midnight, Molly Avery, still too excited about Kent's ten hour ago marriage proposal (and her acceptance) to sleep, decided to go clean the church now instead of in the morning before service. She had intended to get it done before work, but then Kent had called and, well… July was her month to clean the church, and she had committed to do it and do it well. But she certainly wouldn't be sorry to see August in a week and a half. Especially now that she was engaged.

Engaged! She couldn't get enough of the word.

She drove slowly along the empty streets toward the church, not wanting to draw attention to herself. More specifically, to her expired plates. She'd have to take care of that.

Monday.

Parking right near the church's back door, Molly dug in her purse for her key, hurried inside, and locked the door behind herself. The building was located in an as-yet-to-be fully developed upper-class section of town, but had been vandalized recently, probably at this time of a night very much like this one. She wasn't about to take any chances now that she was engaged.

She smiled. That word again.

As she vacuumed classrooms and absently scrubbed nursery toys in warm soapy water, Molly thought about weddings. *Her* wedding, specifically. She and Kent walking down the aisle of the beautiful sanctuary where she had spent almost every Sunday morning of her life. Twenty-six years worth of Sunday mornings. Kent was not a Christian, not a declaring one anyway, but he'd promised her the church wedding she'd always dreamed of.

While considering colors that would match or at least not clash with the church's new mauve carpeting, she remembered something Pastor Corelli had preached recently. She recalled tenacity in the new pastor's eyes as he'd said, "That's why we stand against abortion. That's why we don't cheat on our taxes even though the IRS might never know the difference. That's why, as a pastor, I will no longer marry a believer to an unbeliever." He had gone on, earning everyone's attention and a lot of respect, including Molly's.

But now...

Will he marry Kent and me?

Molly was certain she could find another pastor to perform the ceremony, or a Justice of the Peace, if worse came to worse...but would Pastor Corelli let her use the building?

Surely he would.

Right?

Molly wondered. The man was still too new to be predictable. And she had been so preoccupied with her relationship with Kent that her mind had done a lot of wandering during most of the services since Pastor Corelli's arrival. She didn't know him at all, she realized. But she did know that this was her church. She had always dreamed of having her wedding *here*. Could a man who hadn't even been here six months rob her of that dream just because her fiancée didn't have time for religion?

She couldn't stand the thought of it!

In her growing anger she nearly decided not to clean his office. He wasn't going to be at church in the morning, anyway. But then she relented, figuring it would be better to stay on his good side—assuming he had one.

His office was meticulous, as always. She vacuumed the floor, dusted the family pictures on his book shelf, and smiled in spite of herself when she turned to his desk. *A stack of papers. So he is human!* She picked up the stack to straighten it, though it really didn't need straightening, and from somewhere in the middle a sheet of yellow legal paper slipped out and fell to the floor.

Molly bent to pick it up, not actually intending to look at it…

"Pastors to contact for possible pastors' prayer" had been written neatly on the top line.

Interesting, Molly thought, until she scanned the list. Fifteen or twenty names followed by the names of their churches with their affiliation or denomination marked in a third column.

"Isn't that kind of controversial?" Molly said to the empty office.

She read the rest of the list. Three evangelical-type churches. A few main-line denominations. And…*what?*

Four "Pentecostal" or "charismatic" pastors!

Molly had heard Pastor Corelli defend their church's beliefs regarding the so-called spiritual gifts and their place in the early church, so why would he want to pray with men who believed in them, in *tongues*, for today?

Maybe this was just a first draft and Pastor Corelli had yet to trim the list down to an appropriate prayer group?

Molly hoped so. Because if this man was going to forbid her to marry Kent in her church building and then go pray with people who spoke in tongues, well, that would be too much! Way too much.

* * *

Pastor Alec Hale awoke at the sound of a single gunshot.

Across the lake.

Quickly he pulled on his boots and felt around his sleeping bag for his flashlight. *What are those boys doing?*

He had seen the two boys arrive at the lake earlier that evening and set up their camp. After being alone at the lake all week fasting, he had enjoyed hearing their laughter even if it had been accompanied by a bit of whining about the long and uphill seven miles in. He hadn't thought to be particularly worried about them, though they couldn't be too much older than his own son. He'd figured that, like his son, these boys had learned to handle themselves up here.

And he'd taught his son never to fire a weapon in camp unless...

He scrambled out of his tent, ran straight to the inlet to cross over to the other side of the lake, and hurried toward the sound of one of the boys telling the other again and again that everything was going to be okay.

The other boy wasn't making any noise, and that

didn't sound too much like *okay* to Alec Hale.

When he got close enough for the boys to hear him, he shouted, ""What's going on? Do you need some help?" He wanted them to know that he was coming and that he was a *he* and not an *it*. The flashlight should give that away, but if the boys were panicked, if they'd just seen a griz, they might fire first and wonder how a bear got a flashlight later.

"It was a wolverine, I think," the boy doing all the talking shouted to him. "It attacked Justin!"

A wolverine? Alec had never seen a wolverine in these mountains, but he knew they lived here. And he had heard stories about them. The way they'd climb to the roof of a settler's cabin, go down the chimney, and kill everyone inside. The way they'd hide in trees and pounce on unsuspecting animals below. The way they could kill a moose—an animal that far outweighed its fifty or sixty pounds.

Alec knelt with the boy who had stood to meet him and helped him tighten and tie a strip of cloth around the other boy's right upper arm, just above where the animal had clearly latched on. "Did you shoot it?"

"No. I…it was all over Justin and I… " The boy swallowed hard. "I just shot. To scare it off him. Up, I think."

"All right," Alec said. "It might still be around so we're going to have to be careful."

The boy nodded.

Alec found no other serious bites or scratches. Justin was conscious and alert, though frighteningly still and quiet. His breathing seemed normal enough, but Alec didn't take much comfort in that because the boy had lost a lot of blood. He knew that things could go downhill very quickly so he wasted no time about considering his options and making a decision.

"They might not be able to get a helicopter up here in the dark," he said to the other boy, "and anyway, with that wolverine out here, I'm not too comfortable about leaving you here with him while I go for help." He paused. "What kind of packs have you got?"

"Sir?"

"Internal frames?"

The boy understood. "No. I'll go get them."

After tying the two pack frames together as a make-do stretcher and wrapping one of the sleeping bags tightly around Justin to keep him warm and secure him, Alec and the other boy quickly but carefully, with ears alert to the trees around them, made their way down the steep trail.

2

When Alec's son Jon got out of bed the following Tuesday morning at 7:30 and saw nothing but blue sky through his open bedroom window,
he decided that the day couldn't be better to hike up
to the lake, pack up his father's camping gear, and
bring it back home for him, carrying concentrated
pepper spray in case he ran into the wolverine that
had attacked the boy his father had rescued.

As always, Jon was proud of his father. He had
known exactly what to do for that injured boy and he
had done it, in spite of his own physical weakness
after a week of fasting. And the kid was going to be
all right. In fact, he'd left the hospital with his
friend's parents before his own parents could even
get back to town. Jon's only regret was that he
hadn't been there himself. He could have helped his
father. And he would like to have met the kid who
his father knew only as *Justin*. Jon figured he never

would meet him, though, since his father, in all the confusion at the emergency room, hadn't learned his last name and had been denied that information later by a semi-rude hospital employee who kept citing some rule about patient confidentiality.

Oh well. Jon was plenty content with knowing that Justin was going to be fine and that his hiking up to the lake today would be a big help to his father. He would have preferred to hike up, do some fishing, spend the night, and then hike out, but Dad had responded to that idea with enough quiet reluctance to convince Jon to settle for a day hike. A long, fifteen mile, day hike. But he was a runner. He could handle it. No sweat. And he'd even thought of the perfect person to ask to join him since his father had to get back to the church and couldn't go.

Another runner. Will Cooper.

Jon dressed quickly, ate breakfast while he packed a lunch and filled his canteens, and then climbed into his pickup and headed for Will's house. He hated to drop in on people without calling first, but the Coopers didn't have a phone. Will's father hated interruption and loud ringing. Jon had always gotten the impression from Will that his father hated a lot of things. Including his son. But Will didn't talk much about his father and Jon didn't press him. If Will was going to open up at all, it was going to be when he was ready. Not before. And Jon wasn't interested in offending him by trying to pry it out of him.

When Jon pulled into the Coopers' driveway, he was relieved to see Will's truck there and Mr. Cooper's car gone. Jon had never met Will's father, and, for today at least, he was not disappointed to be leaving it that way. He took the porch steps two at a time and rang the doorbell.

While he waited he noticed, not for the first time, the almost obsessive and perfect arrangement of the furniture on the porch. It always looked as if nobody ever sat in it and wasn't welcome to, either. The porch was swept, and the vase on the wicker table held fresh flowers. *Strange*, Jon thought, *for a place where two men lived alone.*

"Who is it?" came Will's voice from the other side of the wood door.

"Jon."

A long silence and then the lock clicked and the door opened. Slowly, and only halfway. "What's up?" Will asked him.

Jon noticed the bruises on the left side of Will's face right away, but didn't say anything about them because Will was clearly trying to hide them by standing behind the door. "I have to do some hiking today," he said. "Want to come?"

"How far?" Will wanted to know.

"About fifteen miles."

A pause. "Will we be back by 10:00? I have to be back by 10:00."

"As long as you don't wimp out on me and need to rest every five minutes."

Will smiled. "I'll go get my boots. Come in."

Inside the house, Jon again sensed an oddness in the untouchable feel of the room. Its furniture and its forced order. It looked phony. Like a room set up and created just to be pictured in a women's magazine.

And there was nothing to indicate that it was really more than that. No family pictures. No newspaper tossed on the floor beside the recliner. Nobody's unfinished glass of orange juice on the coffee table.

Weird.

Especially since Mr. Cooper was a construction worker. Jon had a hard time understanding how a man could be comfortable in the mess of a house under construction *and* in the flawlessness of this house. Two extremes. *Mr. Cooper must be one tough puzzle to figure out every day,* Jon thought…and then he wondered what happened when Will failed to figure it out.

When Will came downstairs, unable now to hide his face, Jon asked, "What happened, Will?"

"Don't ask."

It wasn't the kind of *don't ask* that people use when they really do want you to ask so they can whine at you about the answer. It was the *I don't want to tell you, and I don't want to lie, and you really don't want to know, anyway* kind of *don't ask.*

So Jon didn't ask.

"We have to be home by 10:00," Will said again, looking at Jon.

"We will be. Relax." Then Jon thought of something. "Saturday night when you left the coffeehouse, it was way past ten."

Will nodded.

"Did you get in trouble?"

"I woke up my father. But I don't want to talk about it. If that's not okay with you, Hale, I'm staying home. Fifteen miles is too long to…"

"It's okay with me," Jon assured his friend. "I won't ask any more questions." He paused. "Today."

"Good enough." Will tapped his baseball cap against the heel of his other hand a few times. "So are we going, or what?"

"We're going."

As he led the way outside and to his truck, Jon wondered if he might be failing Will somehow by letting the issue go so easily. He knew he'd be telling himself all day that Will could have bruised his face playing football, or by walking into an open cupboard door, or by tripping over the shoe that would never be on the floor in his house and falling down the stairs.

Telling himself and not believing.

But he had given Will his word. No questions.

Jon figured he had all the answers he needed anyway, and knew that, no matter what, he'd get Will home by 10:00. Before 10:00.

* * *

"Well, you're welcome to come if you change your mind."

"I won't," said the man on the other end of the line and hung up.

Pastor Paul Corelli stared at his telephone for several seconds before setting down the receiver and leaning back in his chair, disappointed. This morning had not gone at all as he had hoped it would, and he was finding little comfort in the fact that he probably should have expected the response he had gotten.

Because he had dared to expect more.

The men were pastors, after all.

How is the world ever going to see Jesus in His church if its pastors can't even pray together?

He had called 16 of the 17 men on his Pastors' Prayer list. It made sense to him that if pastors of different denominations and doctrines prayed together they might begin to understand one another and learn to work together to reach the unsaved in their common community. And that instead of appearing to be the leaders of many different churches, they could truly function as the many members of Christ's one Body.

The same gospel united them, didn't it? The same commission?

What was so horribly wrong with thinking that maybe they could all play on the same team?

A lot, apparently.

Paul stood, rubbed his temples where they ached, and walked past his open office door into the sanctuary. Sometimes he could think more clearly in the sanctuary.

Most of the pastors had been polite to him, assuring him that they would pray about his invitation.

Paul closed his eyes. He didn't want to become critical. People, pastors included, had every scriptural right to choose associates carefully.

The first three men Paul had called pastored charismatic churches. He had phoned them first because, right or wrong, he had assumed that his biggest battle would be with them. The first man had politely said, "No, thank you." The second man would pray about it and get back to him. And the third man...he had angered Paul. So much so that Paul hadn't even bothered to call the fourth and final pastor of that doctrinal persuasion.

"I will not waste my time praying in an environment where the Spirit is not free to move," the man had told Paul before quoting I Thessalonians 5:19-20 in a loud, arrogant, and extremely condescending tone.

Paul had replied calmly. "Sir, I take offense at your presumption that the Spirit would not be free to flow." He had wanted, so wanted, to ridicule the man for his more probable concern that his *tongue* might not be free to flap, but he had held his peace.

Yes. Pastor Smith had made him angry. But Paul understood that it was the man's insolence that had injured him, not his doctrine. Pride, Paul knew, could make even the most accurate position ugly, which was demonstrated all too adequately by a few of his fellow cessationists when he had called them.

"Paul," one of them had said, a friend, "what are you thinking? What will you do when one of them wants to start prophesying?"

"Pastor Corelli," another had said, "those people aren't even Christians! Why would you want to include them?"

Several others had mentioned demons, false gospels, psychosomatic babble.

So, for all Paul's prayer and effort—and hope, he had 13 definite *no*'s, 3 *I'll get back to you*'s, and one man he hadn't had the fortitude to call. Apparently, at least in this town, unity was a great idea if you wanted to sell a book, but that was all. Something that everyone wanted to talk about but very few people wanted or knew how to do.

Paul forced himself to stop thinking about it. His fretting about the disquieting power of the issue of the Baptism of the Holy Spirit (and its past or present evidences) to divide Christ's church wasn't going to improve the situation. He needed to relax. To get his mind on something else.

And he knew exactly the thing.

After glancing at his watch and seeing that he still had an hour and a half before his first counseling session that afternoon, he left the church and headed straight for Vern's Tackle Shop.

The business sat on the side of a hill at the edge of town. Signs in the windows advertised what the place was famous for—Vern's home-tied flies. Vern sold packaged flies, of course, and lures, bobbers, hooks, poles, vests, waders, live bait, and everything else a guy could ever use fishing, but it was his own flies that reeled in fishermen.

The building itself was nothing to look at. Log with a tin roof. A gravel parking area right off the side of the highway. No exit. No sign. You had to know what it was or you'd drive right by it. One of the board members of Paul's church had shown it to him.

"You have to go before 2:00," the board member had told Paul, "or Vern won't be there. Fishes every day."

Paul had been skeptical about the success of a business run this way, but apparently people in this part of the country didn't mind arranging their schedules around an old man's fishing plans. Customers were always in the store, secretly hoping, Paul suspected, that Vern would maybe invite one of them to join him for the afternoon.

Paul raised his hand to Vern, a man in his sixties with a build consistent with the lifestyle of hiking to and around the most out of the way and lonesome high mountain lakes. The smell of the spray Vern used on his flies, which he worked on behind the counter as he swapped fishing tales with anyone who'd listen, permeated the small building. Like the smell of vinyl in a new car.

"Hey, Preach," Vern called, smiling at Paul. "How's your boy?"

"He's good," Paul replied. "Thanks. I'm looking for a new reel."

"You know where they are," Vern said.

Paul nodded, smiling a little. His high-pressure sales friends in New York would have fits if they could see the way Vern did business. And that it worked!

After ten or fifteen minutes of comparing, Paul went to the counter with the reel he had chosen and a few lures. He waited beside a tall man wearing a business suit who looked like he could run ten miles without breathing hard. Always the short guy in the class or on the team (or anywhere, it seemed), Paul had spent his life directing his efforts away from sports. But since moving west, he was genuinely gaining an appreciation for the great outdoors. For fishing, in particular.

"That everything?" Vern asked the tall man.

"I think so."

Vern waved his hand between Paul and the other man. "You two know each other?"

The two men glanced at one another and then shook their heads. Why would they know each other? The tall, athletic type and the short-but-sharp pastor type.

Vern shrugged and grunted. "Huh. I figured all you guys knew each other." He laughed. "I guess it ain't like the old days when everyone went to church. Must be competin' for the few who do, huh?"

"You lost me, Vern," the other man admitted.

But Vern had not lost Paul. The man beside him must be in the ministry. Was he one of the men Paul had spoken with that morning? Paul remembered his conversation with Pastor Smith and prayed that this man was not him.

"Preach, meet Preach," Vern said.

Paul looked up at the man beside him, held out his hand, introduced himself, and told him which church he pastored.

The man nodded as he shook Paul's hand. "Good to meet you. I'm Alec Hale."

Paul recognized the name immediately. The charismatic pastor he hadn't called.

Pastor Alec Hale waited while Paul paid for his things and then walked out of the store with him. "Ever fly fish?" he asked.

"No," Paul said. "You?"

The man smiled. "You bet. Would you like to try it sometime?"

Paul confessed that he didn't know much about

fly fishing.

The two men talked for several minutes, agreeing to maybe get together for a day trip. And then, as Pastor Hale was saying goodbye and climbing into his muddy vehicle, Paul remembered Pastors' Prayer.

"Pastor Hale," he said, "I…"

"Alec."

"Alec…I'm trying to organize a pastors' prayer meeting." He explained to Pastor Hale that he had contacted several pastors representing most of the Christian denominations in town about meeting together for prayer. He briefly described his vision of many churches working together to better impact the lost in the community. He concluded by saying, "We don't all see eye to eye on every doctrine, but I was thinking that if we endeavored to understand each other, maybe…" He shrugged, mentally preparing for another rejection.

"That's a pretty bold undertaking," Pastor Hale said easily. "What kind of comments did you get?"

Paul told him.

The other man was quiet a moment. "Wouldn't Vern have a field day with that?"

"To our shame," Paul said.

"Mmm. Do you mind if I ask where you stand on the issue of the Baptism of the Holy Spirit, since that seems to be the major stumbling block to your idea?"

Paul told him.

Pastor Hale was quiet again. Thoughtful. Then he shrugged and said, "I'll be there. Why not? If it doesn't work, we've lost nothing. If it does…"

"It seems to me we gain a whole lot," Paul

finished.

"Exactly. Friday morning, you said?"

Paul nodded. "We might be the only two there."

"Well," said Pastor Hale, "if so, and if we're still speaking when we're finished, I'll take you fly fishing afterwards. If you've got the afternoon free."

"I'll schedule it open," Paul promised.

* * *

Ed Cooper was not a happy man. Not only because his job had him on a roof today, sweating in the ninety-four degree heat of the ever present sun with tar burning his knees through his jeans and the pounding around and below him amplifying the thudding that was already beating the insides of his brain. No. The thing that made the day bad was that this was just another in a blurred and seemingly beginningless routine of bad days.

No high points. Ever.

He had been so beaten by so many bad days, he realized as he wiped sweat from the back of his neck with his already soaked handkerchief, that he had actually forgotten how it felt to be anything but miserable.

Drinking helped some, he guessed, but not really. He always ended up feeling worse than when he was sober. Alcohol's failure to really make him forget was beginning to taste like betrayal.

He trusted it, counted on it, needed it to make him forget.

It used to, didn't it?

He couldn't remember.

He thought it did, though, and that had always been good enough.

But not now.

Even in the midst of the confusion and rage that had crippled his mind as he'd stumbled to the sink the other night to wash Will's blood off his hands, he'd known, as he'd always known, that his hatred wasn't going to change anything or improve anything.

Sarah was dead. Yesterday. Tomorrow. Always.

And when Ed had looked at his son the other night, picking himself up off the floor, he'd seen for the first time a man staring up at him. Not a frightened child with tears in his eyes. A man whose eyes reflected his own hate.

When had this happened?

How many years had…?

Years. So many.

Years that could have been so different if——

Ed shoved the thought back. Later. After work. When he could drink.

Why do you keep running back to that liar? Ed asked himself this question even as its answer, another question, hurried into his mind. *Where else can I go?*

Ed Cooper finished out the work day. Pounding in roof shingles to the empty rhythm of his sweltering anger. And then he went home. Maybe he wouldn't drink tonight. Maybe he would cook dinner and sit in front of the television for the evening news. Maybe he and Will could—

No!

Will was the enemy. Always had been. And now that he, too, had grown to hate, Ed knew that this was unchangeable.

Just like everything else in his life.

So, as he walked through his front door and past all the furniture that hadn't been moved since his last morning with Sarah all those years ago, he stopped asking himself *Where else can I go?* and went straight to where he always went.

* * *

When she heard Pastor Corelli come in the front door, Kyra Gress boxed up the game she, Justin, and his younger sister Jessica had just finished playing and stood to leave. Justin was looking tired, and she had to get home to help Mom with supper.

"You don't have to go just because I'm home," Pastor Corelli said when he met her in the family room doorway. Then, smiling, he tossed something to Justin. "Picked this up for you today."

Kyra watched Justin study his new fishing reel, enjoying his obvious pleasure with it. He'd had a rough couple of days. "Corey and I are hiking up tomorrow to get the tent and stuff," she said.

"Oh yeah?" Justin set his reel on the coffee table and looked up at her. "Do you think the guy who helped us down has gone for his yet?"

"Hard to say," she said. "Why?"

"Well, if he hasn't, could you leave a note on his tent for me?"

"Sure."

"I'd like to thank him," Justin said. "I didn't do that. You could leave him our number and a message to call us?"

"Good idea," said Pastor Corelli.

Kyra nodded. "Corey feels really bad about not thinking to ask the guy's name," she said. "So do Mom and Dad. They were scared."

"And it was 2:00 in the morning," Justin said.

Kyra pulled her braid over her left shoulder and redid the clip at its tip. "Corey says he's pretty sure the man was a Christian." This earned Pastor Corelli's attention, so she added, "He talked about God a lot, he said."

"He did," Justin remembered. "I hope his tent's still there so you can leave the note."

"If not," Kyra said, "Corey thinks he'd recognize his outfit again if he saw it. Blue SUV."

Pastor Corelli raised his eyebrows and stared for a moment at her as if what she had just said had connected with something in his brain. Reminded him of something. But then he shrugged and said, "Lots of those around here."

That was definitely true.

Mrs. Corelli joined them then with soup for her son and a concerned expression for Kyra. "Did you say you were going up there with Corey tomorrow, dear?"

Kyra smiled and nodded. She loved Mrs. Corelli's New York accent—though she'd thought it strange at first that she had such a pronounced one since Justin, Jessica, and their father seemed to have none at all. Justin had explained to her that his mother was from Brooklyn but the family had actually lived upstate most of the time, where most people spoke like the rest of America. She said, "Yes. I'm going with him."

"That's a long way, isn't it?" Mrs. Corelli pressed. "Fifteen miles or so, in and out?"

"Yeah."

All four of the Corellis were now staring at her.

"What?" she challenged. "You don't think I can do it? I've been hiking around in these mountains since…" She shut her mouth. They had heard that line before. Recently. Kyra could understand Pastor and Mrs. Corelli's reaction. They were parents. It was their duty to worry and overreact. Especially since their son had nearly had his arm ripped off by a wolverine. And especially since they were from the city, where nobody walked any farther than to and from their car for fear of being mugged.

But Justin and Jessica? They knew that she could hike, boat, climb, or swim anywhere her big brother could. And Justin in particular shouldn't need to be reminded of just who had won when she, he, and Corey had dared one another to be the first to cross the lake or buy the pizza.

In some ways, it amazed Kyra that she and her brother had grown so close to Justin in only six months. To each other. And to God. All the religion stuff she had always heard began to come together for her when she saw another person her own age living his Christianity. Justin loved God. That's it. Plain and simple. No games. No hype. No acting because he was a pastor's kid. He just flat-out wanted to do right by God. And it had rubbed off on many of the other kids in their youth group, including and especially Kyra and Corey.

At first. Kyra had had a stupid and girlish crush on Justin. Because he was a new boy to look at—and not bad to look at, either. And because it seemed romantic, somehow, the idea of him being a pastor's son. She hadn't known what to expect when her father had told her that their new pastor had a sixteen-year-old son. Would he be stuck up? The *I'm better than all of you because my dad is the pastor* thing? Or would he be withdrawn? The *If I blow it it'll ruin my dad's chance for respect here so I better just stay quiet* thing? Justin had surprised and pleased Kyra and just about everyone else by being neither. He had a quick wit, which he knew how, when, and when not to use. His relaxed and genuine personality drew people to him, and he kept them there by being a constant encourager. Kyra had quickly abandoned her crush for the chance at a better and real friendship with him.

A friendship she now treasured.

She grinned at him. "Are you willing to put up a pizza that says I can't make the trail?"

"No way," he said, smiling. Then he told his parents, "She'll make it. No problem."

As Kyra walked home, she reflected that *no problem* was probably a bit of a stretch, but she knew she would make the fifteen-mile hike. And she hoped she and Corey would find the other tent still up there. She'd like to thank the mystery man, too.

* * *

An elderly woman waved at Will Cooper as he climbed the steps to his porch. From her porch she could see, even in the diminishing light of 9:30, bruises on the boy's face.

It's a shame, she thought. *Such a nice and handsome boy.* Brown hair. Hazel eyes. Tall and athletic looking. Several times since her son had bought her this house in town she had thought about calling the police when the shouting started next door.

Mr. Ed Cooper was an evil man. A drunk.

But the woman had been raised to respect a man's privacy in the matter of raising his children, even if she didn't agree with it. Once we started getting the government or anyone else involved in citizens' family lives, nobody would have the freedom to raise their kids the way they saw fit, even decent people. And decent people must have that freedom.

"Where you been?" she heard Mr. Cooper ask the boy, his words running together like too much wet paint on a spilled canvas. As always, she couldn't hear Will's reply. He never yelled back at his father. He was a good boy.

The elderly woman stood, pushed her porch chair up against the side of the house, and went inside to watch television.

It was none of her business.

3

"Dad? Got a minute?"

Alec Hale closed the book he hadn't been able to concentrate on anyway and looked up at his son. "Sure." When Jon had settled into the chair opposite him on the other side of the coffee table, he said, "Thanks for going up for my gear today. I appreciate it."

"No problem."

Sensing an unusual reluctance in Jon, but certain that his son did want to talk about something, Alec attempted some small talk to get the conversation going. "So, did your friend go with you? The boy from the track team. Will, is it?"

"Yeah. Will."

Alec waited through a few minutes of silence from his son and then said, "Jon, what's up?"

"I think Will's father beats him."

Jon had that *There. I said it. Now what?* look in

his eyes, and Alec wasn't sure how to respond to it. "You think…or you know?"

"I think."

"Has he said anything to you?"

"No, but…" Jon described bruises, Will's strange silence concerning his father, his urgency about being home by 10:00, Mr. Cooper's drinking, and his own undecided feelings about the orderliness of the Cooper house. Then he said, "I don't know anything for sure, Dad. I just…something's weird."

"Have you asked him about it?" Alec asked.

Jon shrugged. "In roundabout ways. He always cuts me off. Says he doesn't want to talk about it."

Alec thought back to his first year in the ministry. He'd counseled a man who had physically abused his children, and details of their conversations, and conversations with the man's three children, still haunted Alec when he allowed himself to remember. But he had also counseled a man whose family had nearly been destroyed by a false accusation of abuse. He said, "Jon, you don't want to jump to conclusions about a thing like this. Try talking to him. Maybe ask him what he and his dad do together for fun. Things like that. Maybe he'll open up to you. Until then, you have to be careful not to…" He stopped. "This isn't what you want from me, is it?"

Jon did not reply.

"You've already thought it through this far, and you wanted me to say, 'Okay, now, do this, this, this, this, and that and it'll all be better.'" He smiled. "Am I right?"

Jon nodded.

"That worked when you were six and your big worry was proving to Josh that it wasn't you who stole his baseball cards."

Now Jon smiled, too. "You remember that?"

"Yes. But now, Jon, I don't always have the fix-all answer. Some things just take time and prayer. The best advice I can give you is James 1:5-6."

"*'Now if any of you lacks wisdom...'*"

Alec stood and slid the chess board from the top shelf of the family entertainment cabinet. "Exactly. Want to play?"

"I guess."

After losing the first game, Alec mentioned his conversation with Pastor Corelli.

Jon grinned, holding his rook in the air about six inches above the board. "It's about time you pastor-types started getting current," he said. "Another game?"

"Sure. What do you mean?"

They began to reset the pieces.

Jon shrugged. "You know how God has been slowly, over the centuries, restoring His church to what it was originally? Salvation by grace. Water baptism. The gifts of the Spirit." He looked steadily at Alec. "Lots of guys think that unity is His next big move."

"Guys at your coffeehouse?" Alec asked, not sure he'd be convinced by a few zealous high school and college kids, though of course Christ would want unity in the church.

"Yeah, but not just them. People are writing books and stuff." Jon moved one of his pawns and then looked up at Alec. "Your move."

"Yeah." Alec slid one of his own pawns forward. "How does it work at the coffeehouse, Jon? You've got people there from just about every Christian church imaginable, right? Do you all get along?"

"Mostly," Jon said quietly. "To tell you the truth, Dad, and I never would have figured it to be this way before we got started with it, I actually get along better with the kids who don't believe in the gifts of the Spirit for today than with some of the other Spirit-filled kids that show up there."

"Why?" Alec asked, no longer interested in chess but moving his bishop out just to perform his turn.

Jon moved his own bishop but didn't pay too much attention to where he set it down. "Because some of them are, well, weird. Casting demons out of everyone and everything, including Christians. Blaming every sin in their life on some kind of generational curse, or something. It gets on my nerves. They're the loud ones so everyone thinks that's what all charismatics are like." He looked up at his father. "And we're not."

Alec knew exactly what his son meant. It was equally as ignorant for non-charismatic believers to suppose that all charismatics behaved inappropriately in respect to the spiritual power available to them as it was for charismatics to believe that all non-charismatics were altogether dead in matters of the Spirit. Because he understood Jon's frustration so well, and because of Pastor Corelli's invitation that morning, Alec asked, "But you do work together, right?"

"Yeah. We work together." Jon smiled. "It's when

all the unsaved people have gone home that we have all our problems."

"Like?" Alec forgot all about the chess game.

Jon didn't mention that it was his father's turn. "Like, Joey'll say, 'Man, couldn't you see that that guy needed a demon cast out of him big time? Why'd you interrupt me when I started to pray for him?' And then Rachel'll say, 'He didn't need any demon cast out! He just needs to quit getting drunk.' Then, Todd'll say, 'Don't be so legalistic, man. Jesus loves the dude just the way he is.'" Jon laughed. "Then, inevitably, someone'll say, 'What do you guys think about Christians going to bars and drinking pop, you know, to witness?'" Jon remembered the chess game and pointed at his father. "Your turn."

"Oh yeah. Sorry." Alec moved his queen. "But you guys are still friends when you leave, right?"

Jon nodded.

"And when you're witnessing, you're all together?"

"Yeah."

"And that goes okay?"

"Yep." After a few seconds of thought, Jon placed his knight to threaten Alec's queen.

Alec returned his queen to her original position. "What do you do when someone gets saved and wants to know where to go to church?"

"Mostly," Jon said, "a guy will respond to one person in the conversation more than to anyone else. We've agreed that whichever of us has established that link, I guess you'd call it, that person will invite him."

"That's diplomatic," said Alec.

"Well, could you imagine someone just getting saved and then sitting around to watch while we all slammed each other's churches?"

Unfortunately, Alec didn't have to imagine. He had seen it happen. In fact, he had done it. But only once. In his case, shame and regret had been excellent teachers. Alec was glad to see his son learning such a valuable thing from a different, easier teacher.

A quiet knock at the front door startled Alec, and Jon, too. They laughed it off though as Alec stood, glanced at the clock on the wall, crossed the living room, and pulled open the door.

Both of them stopped laughing.

"Will? What...?"

Alec stepped back so that Jon could go to his friend, take gentle hold of his arm, and lead him inside. Then he closed the door and turned to look at the boy.

He was holding his hand over his left eye, but Alec could clearly see bruising there. And blood.

"I'm sorry," Will said, first to Jon and then to Alec. "I didn't know where else to go. Jon said I could come here if I ever needed somewhere to go."

"Go get your mother," Alec said to Jon and then led Will to the couch and sat beside him. Looking straight at him, he asked, "Who did this to you?"

Will stared at his knees and said nothing.

Deciding that this was a time to press, Alec said, "Whether you tell me or not, Will, you're welcome to stay here tonight. And, if this happens again." He glanced at Will for some kind of signal that he was heading in the right direction, but the boy kept his eyes down. "If this happens again, we'll help you again, if that's what you need. But I'd like to try to help you more than by cleaning up your face and giving you a safe place to sleep."

Will nodded.

"Will, who did this to you?" Alec asked again, gently, and then waited while the young man beside him struggled with what had to be a torrent inside himself. With a decision of whether or not to trust.

Finally he answered. "My father."

* * *

Because of Pastor Paul Corelli's invitation, and more than that, because of what it hoped to accomplish, several pastors lay awake that night beside their wives. Three of them had yet to give the man an answer.

Pastor Al Snyder had no intention of participating in Pastor Corelli's little prayer group. He had lost nearly all the young families in his congregation to pentecostal churches. They liked the modern music—which Al considered of satanic origin and totally out of place in the house of God. They enjoyed the more animated preaching styles of charismatic pastors. And, of course, the emotional ecstasies of a "Spirit Filled" service attracted and kept them. Al hated the charismatic movement and everything it produced in the lives of those who fell prey to its deceptive but appealing promises. Spiritual Power. Prosperity. Divine Health. Supernatural Experiences With God.

Etc. Al didn't buy it. He considered it a scheme from Hell itself and would never pray with anyone who led otherwise good believers into such heresy and ultimately out of the fold.

But Pastor Snyder certainly did not wish to appear to be standing in opposition to Christian unity when Christ's impassioned prayer in John 17 made His desire for it abundantly clear.

So, he lay awake, wondering if he might perhaps reschedule his weekly men's Bible study to the day and hour of the week that Pastor Corelli had suggested for his supposed prayer meeting. Or, if maybe this was God's way of telling him that now was the time to begin that nursing home ministry he'd always planned to look into someday.

He'd find something.

Also awake, but praying more than thinking, Pastor Terry Stoltz labored over his decision. He was all for the idea, but he'd mentioned it in passing to one of his board members and the man had erupted in such a tirade of "I'll be stone cold dead before a pastor of mine prays with tongue-talkers and...you weren't thinkin' about it, were you, Pastor?" that Terry had grunted noncommittally and changed the subject.

But now, in the dark of night, Terry was powerless against the subject.

Church politics. They had to be the worst thing for the Church. But what could he do? His board owned more power in his church than he did. Basically, he was their pawn. Their chaplain more than their spiritual leader. If he appeased them, he kept his house and job. If he crossed them, the denomination had plenty of other churches. Smaller churches. In smaller places.

Not Terry's idea of a brilliant career move.

Besides, he'd grown to love *this* church. He seemed to be able to reach its people with his hope and burden for a full life in Christ and they responded back to him. Not every pastor could say that. But a congregation's respect could be easily lost these days, and Terry was confident that his embracing of Pastor Corelli's vision, since charismatics had been invited, might just be too much for his people. At this point, anyway.

Terry decided that he wasn't willing to risk it. What good would participation in pastors' prayer do him if he ceased to be a pastor because of it? He'd call Corelli first thing in the morning. The man would certainly understand his dilemma. Corelli had a church board, too.

At last, with his decision made, Terry Stoltz rolled onto his side and closed his eyes for some much needed sleep.

But it didn't come.

Neither would it come for Pastor Mel Pearson. Impressed as he was that a non-Spirit-filled man would invite him to pray with him, Mel just couldn't see it leading to anything but conflict. What pastor needed any more of *that* than he already had?

Since the revival that had recently swept through his church, Mel's congregation had been torn. Half of them thinking that Mel had allowed things to get too weird. Laughter. Weeping. People being "slain" in the Spirit. Evening services that didn't let out until well after midnight. Dancing. And the other half of his congregation thinking that Mel was stifling the Spirit. Preaching a sermon at every meeting instead of letting the Spirit lead. Refusing to acknowledge the woman who came in the door for the first time with a vision that *she* was really the chosen one to be pastoring his church.

Conflict.

Mel certainly had his fair share of it, and wasn't looking for any more.

Some people in his congregation would probably start casting demons out of him if they knew he was seriously considering praying with noncharismatics!

Mel laughed even though nothing was funny.

How could a bunch of pastors who'd never battled to balance that which was the genuine outpouring of the Holy Spirit with the inevitable tendency of human flesh to embellish it really minister to his needs? How could their prayers for him honestly reach God when those praying would be thinking the whole time that everything he stood for and struggled with was all foolishness, anyway? And, how could he pray for them in the fullness of prayer he had grown to cherish and require without offending them?

As much as Mel Pearson wished and longed for peer support and friendship, he didn't think Pastor Corelli's prayer group was the answer. And as much as he would like to hope and believe that a group of pastors could see beyond doctrinal differences to truly unite in prayer and ministry, he found it impossible to ignore the situation's potential for anger and conflict.

Still, Corelli's endeavor was honorable and commendable. Even if he chose not to pray *with* him, Mel determined to pray *for* him and for the other pastors who decided to accept his invitation. He'd add it to his prayer list in the morning. He hoped he'd remember.

* * *

Moonlight through pale curtains. A cool breeze across his burning face. Silence. Will Cooper lay wide awake, intimidated by the silence in the Hale house rather than comforted by it. He was used to his father's television blaring at him through the wall. Laughter. The occasional outburst at a late-night talk show host. Will had learned to find safety in the noise from his father's room. As long as it stayed on the other side of his closed door.

The door to his room here, the Hales' guest room, was open. And everywhere, the whole house was still. So still that Will could hear the hum of the streetlamp outside. He'd always wondered what it would be like to sleep in a normal house. A house where people slept at night. A house with a mother and father, maybe a couple of brothers and sisters down the hall. A house where he didn't need to be afraid.

Well, this was definitely that house, but Will still couldn't sleep.

His ribs hurt where his father had kicked him.

Pastor Hale was going to go talk with his father tomorrow. One of those 'You either agree to counseling or I go straight to the powers that be that punish men like you" conversations, and Will was worried about how it would go. Would his father agree to counseling? Or would he kill Will for telling?

Mostly, though, Will lay awake because of the words his father had spit in his face tonight. Words that had sent him running from his house, for the first time afraid that he couldn't handle it alone. Words he had been unwilling to repeat to Pastor or Mrs. Hale, or even Jon.

Words his father had never said before.

Words that changed everything.

Now that you're a man, Will, you should know the truth. You killed your mother. You.

Will pulled his knees to his chest. His stomach hurt.

Will's mother had died when he was three years old. How had he killed his mother? At three years old? Why had his father waited until now to tell him?

His father could be wrong. Putting blame in the wrong place. People did that all the time, right? His father could have flat-out lied. Made a crazy accusation in his drunken rage.

No. His father had known exactly what he was saying. And he clearly believed it.

Could Will have...somehow...?

You killed your mother. You.

A sound in the hallway. A soft light. A gentle touch at the side of his head.

Will jumped, trying not to yell out, fighting an unyielding tenseness in his stomach and burning in his throat and eyes.

"I'm sorry," came a quiet voice. Mrs. Hale. "I

didn't mean to wake you."

"I wasn't asleep," Will mumbled, both angry and relieved that she had interrupted his thoughts.

She sat beside him on the edge of the bed, her hand still touching his hair. Soothing. "I just came to check on you," she said. "Do you need anything? Some hot tea? Aspirin? A warmer blanket?"

"I don't need anything," he said. "Thanks."

She must have been unconvinced, because she didn't leave. "Don't think about it now, Will," she said. "Try to sleep." Then she began talking to him. About her father. Her grandfather. A broken promise. A ruined crop. Years of bitterness. And then Jesus. Her presence beside him relaxed him. Her voice and her words. Until, when he was half awake and half asleep, they seemed to come from everywhere and mean everything.

"Look at the frog, Will."

Mommy lay beside him in the grass, her chin on the curb, right next to his.

Will looked across the gray street and saw the frog hopping out from underneath a car. "He's ugly," he said.

"Yes, he is." Mommy laughed.

"Sarah, I need more nails."

Daddy was building a birdhouse.

Mommy stood and Daddy yelled, "Get away from the street, Will."

But Will was watching the frog. Wondering what it would feel like in his hands. He could find out if he could catch it.

Then he was on his knees in the street, the frog in

his hands, and he began to cry because his father was yelling at him to get out of the street and a loud, loud noise right next to him was hurting his ears, and then...

Hands on his back. Pushing him.

On his face on the sidewalk.

By himself.

But then a lady in a blue shirt came. His head hurt and he felt like he had to throw up. He could hear his father shouting at him, "Why didn't you get out of the street? I told you to get out of the street! You hurt your Mommy! You were a bad boy!" When he turned around to tell his father he was sorry, he saw his mother. In the street. Blood.

"I didn't mean to," Will cried as the lady in the blue shirt picked him up and made him look away. "I'm sorry I was bad. I didn't mean to!"

Will Cooper muttered in his sleep as the long forgotten tears of a three-year-old child wet his bruised face. He didn't know then that the EMT who had held him had wept with him, knowing that no three-year-old child should see his mother lying dead in the street and then hear from the mouth of his father the lie that it was his fault. And he didn't know that Mrs. Hale was weeping with him now, not knowing any details, but convinced that no set of details could justify a father inflicting this kind of pain on his sixteen-year-old child.

Will Cooper knew only that his father had finally told him the truth.

He had killed his mother.

4

When Alec pulled into the parking lot of Pastor Corelli's church the following Friday morning for the first prayer meeting, he had no idea what to expect. He was trying to not approach it any differently in his mind than he did his weekly prayer breakfasts with some of the other charismatic pastors. But it was different, and no amount of mental gymnastics was going to change that fact.

Stepping out of his car, he reviewed the three items he most wanted to pray about this morning. He had spoken to Will Cooper's father earlier in the week. Ed Cooper had reluctantly agreed to counseling. They had met twice already. So far the man had not hit Will again, but he was still drinking. So the situation remained potentially volatile. Unreliable. In need of a breakthrough. A realization of God.

Also, Jon had confided to Alec a couple nights ago that Will had almost completely quit talking to him. He seemed angry. Withdrawn. "Despondent," Jon had said. "Like his father not hitting him is a bad thing." Alec had encouraged his son to keep after Will, to realize that emotions can overwhelm kids in crisis, to constantly remind Will of his friendship. But Alec knew that Will needed more than Jon, or Alec, or even his father. Will needed Jesus.

And third, two more churches in town had been vandalized this week. Obscenities had been spray painted on walls, signs, and sidewalks. And in each case, as with the others, windows had been smashed so that pictures and articles about bombed abortion clinics, the most recently murdered doctors, and the horrors of religious wars past and present in which Christians were the aggressors, could be scattered on the floor inside the church. People had begun to whisper and to be afraid. *Whose church will be next? Why? How long until these people stop targeting buildings and start going after people? Is this somebody's warped idea of a prank? A gang initiation? A genuine hate crime? Why is this happening here? Now?*

Pastor Corelli met Alec inside the sanctuary doors and shook his hand. "Pastor Hale. Thanks for coming."

Alec nodded. "Please. Alec. Are we the only ones?"

Paul gestured grandly with his arm at the empty room. His face held a smile, but his dark eyes showed disappointment. "Looks that way." Then he said, "I was thinking maybe we could spend a couple minutes getting to know a little more about one another, then mention prayer needs, and then pray."

He paused, looking directly at Alec. "Sound okay?"

"Sounds good."

Paul went first. Raised in Upstate New York. Accepted Christ in college. Attended seminary. Moving around for the denomination ever since. Had a church here of about two hundred members.

Then Alec took his turn. Grew up on a ranch in Montana. Accepted Christ in high school. Attended a Bible college. Served as an assistant pastor for six years at a church in Minnesota, and then moved west again to give it a go on his own. No denomination. Just him. It was hard at times, but he believed God had called him to it. His church, too, had grown to about two hundred people.

There was an awkward silence after Alec finished, as Paul seemed to be considering the things he had been told, which Alec dismissed by mentioning his three prayer requests.

Paul wrote them in the notepad he had open on the pew beside him, and then said, "I was in Vern's shop the other day getting some of his insight into fly fishing, and the Lord opened up a huge door for me to witness to him. I basically gave him the entire gospel but stopped short of asking him to make the commitment because he seemed to still need some persuading inside. You know, he was agreeing with me intellectually, but that's as far as it was going." Paul paused and looked at Alec, clearly waiting for some kind of clue that Alec understood.

Alec nodded. He understood perfectly and was pleased to discover such a level of spiritual discernment in a man who believed, doctrinally anyway, that God stopped speaking to His children by any other means than His written Word after the death of the last apostle.

"I want us to pray for him," Paul said, "during the next few days while the Holy Spirit is dealing with him."

Again, Alec nodded. Impressed now as well as pleased. He had tried several times to share the gospel with Vern only to run into the same wall of arguments and put-offs. "I'll definitely pray with you there," he said.

"Also," Paul said, "my son got hurt pretty seriously last week and I want to pray for his continued restoration to full health."

"All right," Alec said, not wanting to go anywhere near the issue of healing. Not today. He was about to ask Paul what had happened to his son when they were interrupted by a phone call, and when Paul returned to the sanctuary several minutes later, he was already mentioning his other prayer needs.

When he sat beside Alec again, Paul looked directly at him and said, "Obviously, Alec, I would prefer if you didn't pray in tongues, but I won't insist that you don't."

Alec cringed inside. *Here it comes.* The only consolation was that Paul had started it and not him. He said, "I don't have to pray in tongues, Paul. The Bible says to pray with the Spirit and with the understanding. I'll pray with the understanding now so we can both be comfortable and I can pray in the Spirit later. When I'm alone."

"Are you saying I don't pray in the Spirit?" The

challenge lay more in Paul's eyes than in his tone, but it lay there plain enough.

"I was talking about me," Alec stammered. "Not about you." *I didn't intend to imply that you don't pray in the Spirit, but since you're stepping on that road, Pastor Corelli, what does Paul mean when he makes a distinction between the Spirit and the understanding? Or maybe that's one of those passages that conveniently doesn't apply to us today?* But Alec stayed silent, choosing to leave it up to Paul to either let this work or make it fail.

"Good enough," Paul said, quietly. "Shall we pray, then?"

Alec nodded.

Both men bowed their heads, but it was several minutes before either of them spoke. Alec suspected that they both had some getting-the-heart-right to do after that last exchange. He knew he did. And after a while, they began to pray. Both men. One after the other. For the things they had mentioned to one another, and for things that just occurred to them as they prayed.

When they finished nearly an hour later, Alec stood and said, "So, did you bring your fishing gear?"

"In my office." Paul smiled. "I'll lock up and meet you outside."

* * *

Everywhere Will Cooper went, he saw mothers with their children. The park. The grocery store. Playing in the yard across the street.

59

That same street.

On television in laundry detergent commercials.

Everywhere.

Even sitting alone in his living room with no pictures to look at and no television on, he saw mothers with their children in his mind. His mother. Himself. That stupid frog. He could not escape the images. They were making him crazy.

He'd have to go run. He had already run that morning. His usual six miles. Now was the wrong time of day for running. Mid-afternoon. Hot. But he didn't care. He ran upstairs, changed into his running clothes and shoes, grabbed his headphone CD player, turned it up as loud as it would go, and ran.

Out the front door.

One mile. Two.

By new houses. The mall.

Three miles.

Past the lot where they parked all the school buses. A Llama farm.

Four miles.

Five.

Sweat soaked his shirt and his earphones, but he kept running.

Six miles.

Then he stopped. Right in front of the last gas station before the road exited onto the eastbound Interstate entry ramp. What was he doing? What was he thinking? He couldn't run away from this. No matter how far he ran, for however long, it would still be there. Inside him. He'd have to chase it out if he wanted to be rid of it.

But how?

As he turned and walked back toward his house, he thought about Jon Hale. His friend. Jon had been after him for days. "Let's do something, Will." Maybe he could go see Jon later and accept his most recent invitation to drive to the waterslide. Maybe Jon could help him deal with this. And, if not Jon, maybe Pastor Hale. He had to get some help. He felt like his life had been chewed up by some giant demon and then spit back out because it wasn't worth eating.

Will began to run again. More slowly than before, more at his usual smooth pace. He loved to run, and he was good at it. A regular winner at distance events. But mostly he ran because it was the one thing in his life that he could control. Its steadiness, its predictability, and its monotony all kept him sane when everything else swerved and crashed at the passing whims of his father's hatred.

But now that he understood that hatred, he needed more than a diversion. He needed answers. He needed peace.

I don't deserve peace. I killed my own mother. I destroyed my father's life. Everything he's done to me, I deserve.

By the time Will reached his house, shame, guilt, and anger, and those images of his mother first beside him and then in the street, had piled down on him again. Smothered him. How could he tell Jon or anyone else what he had done? He couldn't. That's all. He couldn't.

Will had to stand there inside his front door and make himself breathe. If he couldn't go to Jon or

Pastor Hale, or anyone else, where could he go?

I can't handle this. It's too much. I can't handle this!

But where can I go?

Slowly, Will walked into the kitchen, set his CD player on the table, and pulled open the refrigerator door.

He could go where his father always went.

* * *

Shayna Quinn loved to ride in Jon Hale's truck. Loud, fast, and lifted, the teal pickup earned lots of second glances from other drivers, and Shayna couldn't think of anyone she'd rather be seen twice with than Jon Hale.

"I want to stop by Will's to see if he wants to come tonight," Jon said.

Shayna nodded.

It was Friday night. The first coffeehouse night of the weekend. Shayna volunteered at the Christian coffeehouse every time the doors were open because this year, at 16, she had begun to feel a need to establish her faith in Christ as something more than "I'm a Christian because my dad's a church elder and he raised me that way." Working at the coffeehouse, dealing one on one with people in an environment that gently pressured her to "let her light shine" and tell why it was shining had definitely improved her understanding of the terms "lost" and "saved" and of her own capacity to be used by God. It was exciting and powerful. Much deeper, much more than religion. It was reality.

"Do you think he will?" she asked Jon, aware of how committed Jon was to imparting that reality to his friend Will, but just as aware of Will's previous opposition. "You're as stubborn as your father about hanging in there with a person, Jon."

He smiled at her. "Is that a bad thing?"

Her turn to smile. "Definitely not. I just don't want you to be discouraged if he says no again, though he did come last week."

Jon stayed silent until he parked his truck in Will's driveway. "Coming?"

Shayna stepped out of the truck and followed Jon up the porch steps and stood beside him as he rang the doorbell. "Pretty patio furniture," she observed.

A slow nod from Jon.

Will came to the door then, grinning as he said, "You know what? I was thinking about you this afternoon. Weird, huh?"

Shayna stepped back. The smell of beer on Will's breath and the nervous confidence in his eyes sickened and frightened her.

"Will, you're drunk," Jon said.

"Yes sir, I am."

Jon moved closer to Will. Right in his face. "What are you doing, man?"

"Nothing thousands of people our age aren't doing right now as we speak." He laughed, and then burped. "Sorry," he said, laughing again, not sorry at all.

"Where's your father?" Jon asked him.

The changes of emotion evident in Will's behavior, and especially in his eyes, stunned Shayna.

He backed away from Jon, no longer laughing. "He doesn't drink alone on Fridays, Hale," he said. "He's with some guys from work."

He looks scared, Shayna thought.

"Will," Jon said, "you don't drink."

For an instant, Will's face turned angry, but just as quickly it went blank. Revealing nothing. Slowly and with a deliberate effort to force the words out clearly, he said, "Like father, like son."

"No," Jon said. "No. You don't want this." He shook his head and pointed at Will. "You're hiding. You're running." Then he turned to leave. "You're running, man. Come on, Shayna. We're going."

But Shayna didn't follow Jon. Will's eyes held her on the porch. She knew nothing about Will Cooper or his father or the things he was battling with, but she knew that Jon knew, and that his words had somehow been just the right ones. Because Will suddenly looked like he wasn't drunk at all. Like he knew that Jon was right, and like that knowledge was almost as bad as whatever it was that he was running and hiding from. Will looked ready to cave in.

"Come on, Shayna," Jon called to her from the bottom of the porch steps.

"Jon…"

"Let's go!"

But Shayna couldn't leave. Not yet. "Will," she said, looking straight at him, "this isn't the answer."

"He knows that," Jon nearly shouted at her. Then, pushing his hand back through his hair, he climbed the porch steps again and put his hands on Will's shoulders. "Will, when you're ready to get real with this thing, you know where I am." Then he gently tugged at Shayna's arm. "Let's go."

This time Shayna followed him.

They had to get to the coffeehouse.

* * *

Zeke Hudson quietly entered the Christian coffeehouse he'd been told so much about and sat alone at a table near the door. He was here to watch and learn, not talk, and if anyone approached and irritated him, he wanted to be able to get out quickly.

The first thing he noticed—and it surprised him, was that most of the people present were about his age. He wouldn't have suspected that so many kids, with all the hype and hysteria they got fed every day at school, still cared about any of this religion garbage.

They're probably all losers, looking for other losers to date them because nobody else will.

A grin tried to steal his face, but he refused it.

Eventually, the words to the songs playing began to intrude on his thinking. Jesus this. Jesus that. It made him want to vomit, but he refused that, too. Everyone was smiling. Just like he remembered everyone smiling. Always smiling. But Zeke knew that here, just like everywhere else, the smiles were lies. Cover ups. Masks. Religious people were among the most miserable and oppressed. Everyone knew that. Zeke remembered.

"Hi."

Zeke said nothing. He hadn't noticed the kid

coming toward him. Maybe he'd be offended by Zeke's rudeness and go away.

No such luck. The kid sat across from him. "I'm Jon Hale."

Zeke stared at Jon Hale. "So what?"

"So nothing, I guess," Jon said, still smiling. "What's your name? I've seen you at school, haven't I?"

This kid was good. Zeke had to give him that, though he would rather not have. "Joe," he lied indifferently.

"Joe," Jon Hale repeated, probably so he wouldn't forget the name. Religious people liked to remember names. If they remembered a person's name, that person would think they really cared—which they didn't. They wanted to grow a church, or have one more success story to share at gatherings like this one, or were just afraid to show up at God's empty handed. But they never cared.

"I haven't seen you here before," Jon said. "How'd you find out about us?"

Zeke shrugged. It didn't matter. And Jon Hale wouldn't be impressed, anyway. "I found out. That's all." Then he asked, "What are you in this for?"

"What?"

The confusion in Jon Hale's face was gratifying. "This." Zeke gestured around the room, at the people. "What are you in it for?"

"Because I want to help people realize that that emptiness they keep running into inside can only be filled with one thing—one person, actually—Jesus Christ."

"How long did it take you to memorize that?"

Jon Hale smiled even though his irritation was plain enough in the way he'd started tapping his fingers on the tabletop.

Zeke decided to press a little harder. To see what it would take to drag out Jon Hale's true character. "Don't you have a church you can harass people from?"

"You are not a happy person, are you? Some people would never go to a church, so we go to them by providing a place where they feel okay about showing up at. Like you. Would you go to a church?"

"No way."

"But you came here."

"Not for the reasons you think."

Jon Hale nodded, his gray eyes intense and his fingers no longer pounding the table. "I don't care why you came. That's between you and God. The important thing is that you did come."

How compassionate of you, Zeke thought. Then he thought of something else. Something he could almost taste. "Do you go to a church?"

Jon nodded.

"Which one?"

He told him, and added, "My father's the pastor."

"The pastor?" Zeke stood. "That's it. I'm out of here."

But Jon Hale stood with him and grabbed his arm. "Joe," he said, and then paused. "That's not your real name, is it? Well, it doesn't matter. God knows your real name. And He knows why you're so angry. He knows how to lead you past it, but you've got to quit running when He calls to you. You can't outrun Him, and He's not going away." A few seconds of silence as Jon Hale looked at Zeke. Eye to eye. Soul to soul. When he released Zeke's arm, he said, "And you know that."

The back of Zeke's neck went cold with sweat as his mind raced against a memory...a prodding...a...

Lie!

Without saying another word to Jon Hale, Zeke ran from the coffeehouse, out into the night where he felt safe. Where he regained control.

* * *

"You guys, the coolest thing just happened." Jon joined Shayna Quinn and two of the newer coffee-house workers, Mark Sticka and Kyra Gress, behind the snack counter. What he was about to tell them would probably stand hair up on Mark and Kyra's arms and leave them thinking he was even weirder than they already thought he was, but he didn't care. He was too excited not to say anything. "I think God just used me in a word of knowledge."

"A word of knowledge?" Kyra asked.

Shayna nodded. "You don't believe they happen anymore, but we do."

Jon wanted to talk about Joe, not about whether or not words of knowledge still happened. Obviously, they did still happen. He said, "I was talking to this guy I haven't seen here before. He was hostile, almost, and I started thinking I might be wasting my time with him. But then, I don't know.

Nothing like this has ever happened to me before. It was like I could see deeper into him than what he was saying. I just knew stuff that I couldn't just know. Like that he already knows God. That he's running. That God wants to restore him."

"And how exactly did you just know these things, Hale?" Mark asked sarcastically.

"It's called a word of knowledge," Jon said. "It's one of the gifts of the Spirit. It's where God tells you something you couldn't otherwise know. Sometimes it'll be something like, 'There's someone here with scoliosis, and God wants to heal you.' Sometimes…"

"Ooooo," interrupted Mark. "Praise GOOOOOD!"

Jon ignored Mark, figuring that Shayna's disgusted glance would be reprimand enough. "Sometimes it's like what happened to me tonight."

"But," Kyra said, looking thoughtfully at him, "how do you know it's something from God and not just…"

"Too much pizza?" Mark offered.

"Because," Jon said, "pizza doesn't produce ministry."

"Ooooo. Ministry. Praise GOOOOOD!"

"Be quiet," Kyra said, glaring at Mark. Then she turned back to Jon. "So, how did the guy respond to what you said about what God showed you?"

"He left," Jon said. "Fast."

"Sounds like a true miracle to me, Hale," Mark said, laughing. "A mighty touch from God."

"He's being obnoxious, Jon," Kyra said, "but he's right. It really doesn't sound all that glorious like you'd think a supernatural communication from

God would be."

"But don't you get it?" Jon pressed. "He did exactly what God told me he'd been doing. He ran."

"Maybe you just scared him," Mark suggested, serious for the first time. "I'd be scared if someone started spouting 'Thus says the Lord' at me."

"I didn't spout," Jon said, beginning to feel defensiveness tugging at his tongue and attitude. He knew that what had happened was real and supernatural, and he wasn't about to back down or apologize for it.

"Why would God show you something like that when you weren't going to have opportunity to reach the kid with it?"

Sensing that, unlike Mark, Kyra was genuinely curious, Jon answered even though he'd rather be out of this conversation than see it turn into a fight. "I don't know. But God does."

"I guess He does," Kyra said after a while.

Jon thought about the kid he had spoken with, and about his friend Will Cooper. Running, both of them. He wondered how bad they'd let things get, how broken they'd wait to become, before surrendering to God. Then he thought of Proverbs 29:1, and though he tried to avoid the sobering thought that they might wait too long, it pursued him with every certainty of overtaking him. Like fire chasing a man up a mountain.

5

August came in hot and stayed that way, the sky thick with smoke from fires north of them all the way into Canada. Clouds tumbled over the mountains every afternoon but dropped no rain, only lightning, before continuing east, leaving behind copper sunsets. Fields, forests, grasslands...everything that wasn't watered by man lay parched and brittle, waiting, it seemed, to burn.

Though Paul Corelli preferred this hot, dry heat to the sticky and humid heat of New York, he was beginning to understand the potential cost of the difference. Now, three weeks into fire season, he found himself longing for that muggy feeling in the air and the rain it promised.

Staring through his office window at another cloudless morning sky, Paul folded the morning's sermon notes and slid them inside the front cover of his Bible. He had a few minutes before people began arriving for church, and he planned to spend them quietly and alone, stilling his mind. During his first few years as a pastor, his mind had been anything but still during those brief moments between the last glance at the notes and the first handshake in the entryway. *What if I overlook something? Get caught by an embarrassing slip of the tongue? Mispronounce or forget somebody's name? What if I'm wrong? What if people fall asleep while I'm preaching?* But experience had fine-tuned Paul's speaking ability, and he had outgrown nervousness. Still, he needed a pause between sermon preparation and church. For focus. For reflection.

Paul stood near his window, thinking of something Alec had told him Friday morning before prayer.

"If I'm prayed up," he'd said, "and I know that my message is what God has for my church that week, I don't get nervous. But if it's been one of those weeks when I can't focus in prayer, or get too busy, or whatever, and I end up putting a sermon together just because there has to be one, then I get uncomfortable. I'm an all right speaker, I guess, but I don't want my services to be something I put together."

Paul had thought about that statement more than once during the past two days and it still intrigued him. Where he found security in his own ability to communicate effectively, Alec seemed to find a stumbling block. Something he knew he could resort to if he wasn't "prayed up" and probably pull it off, but something he'd rather forego in deference to a specific message from God. While Paul planned his sermons well in advance according to his denomination's yearly schedule of topics, Alec went by nothing but what he "felt" God was "putting on his heart" for his church during any given week.

Personally, Paul preferred an orderly approach to his ministry. He appreciated knowing that he wouldn't over preach any one issue at the expense of others. He could not imagine the suspense of arriving at church Sunday morning with the ever-looming possibility of having to change his whole sermon on the way to the pulpit because he "felt" God "leading" him in a different direction.

And yet, Paul had to admit that the idea had some merit. What if God did have something specific, something current and unique to one congregation, to say? Who would say it if not the pastor?

Well, Paul had run out of time to think about it. For now. It was just another one of those differences between he and his charismatic friend that he'd probably never quite understand. One of many. During the past five weeks, he and Pastor Alec Hale had encountered several differences in the way they thought about and did things. But much more significant than any of those were the things they had discovered that united them. Things that formed the foundation for what was becoming a much needed and unexpected friendship. Things like their shared commitment to not only preach about God, but to live for Him. Their mutual concern that the demands of ministry didn't overpower the needs of their families. The desire for more Christian unity. And, of course, fishing.

Paul left his office and headed to the sanctuary.

People had begun arriving for church.

Strange, God's sense of humor! Who'd have thought that my closest friend in years would turn out to be a charismatic pastor? Paul had to smile and the timing was perfect. He held out his hand to one of his board members. One of the two board members who still weren't sure that Paul was the right man for the church. "Hey, Rick. How are you this morning?"

"All right."

"Only all right?" Paul asked, noting the strained expression on the man's face.

Rick smiled. An obvious effort. "It's probably nothing, Pastor," he said. "I was out driving last night and I saw this group of kids just standing in a church parking lot. With everything that's been going on, you know all the church vandalism, I thought…" He shrugged.

"Could be youth group kids," Paul said. "What time was it?"

"About ten," Rick said. "But I don't think it was youth group kids. The whole place was dark and there were no cars in the lot. Just the kids. I thought about stopping to see what they were up to, or calling the police to check it out, but they weren't doing anything. Just standing there. So I just kept driving."

"What else could you have done, Rick?"

"That's what I told myself all night, Pastor," Rick said. "And it wouldn't be bothering me except that…"

"Except?"

The older man pushed his hands back through

his thinning hair. "That church got hit last night. If it was those kids who did it, and I would have called the police, maybe…"

"Maybe they would have run when they heard the sirens and saved their crime for another time," Paul said. "If the kids you saw were even the ones who did it. Which church?"

Rick told him.

Paul stepped back. *Alec's church.*

"Pastor?" Now it was Rick's turn to look concerned.

"That's a friend's church," Paul explained.

"Oh. Pastor?"

Paul waited. He wanted to hurry and get service started so that he could move things along quickly and get over to Alec's church as soon as he could to help him clean off paint, sweep up shattered glass, and throw away the literature that had undoubtedly been left inside his church, but he didn't want to neglect Rick in the process. "This isn't your fault. Even if the kids you saw were the ones who…"

"They burned the church," Rick said. "To the ground. As dry as it's been, it took a whole field with it before they could put out the fire."

"They *what?*"

Rick did not need to repeat what he'd said.

* * *

Elise Hale stood beside her father, grateful that most of the church members had finally gone home. Their church building had been burned and then drenched and the smell of charred ground and damp ashes sickened her. Her father had built the church twelve years ago, when Elise was two, and now it was gone. A black heap in a black field. All that remained was the black parking lot where they were standing. Her father, her mother, Jon, a couple of the church elders and their families, and a police officer.

Elise refused to cry.

They'd build a new building. That's what insurance was for. She was sick of everyone having to cram into the sanctuary, anyway. Now they could have a bigger building. New chairs. Maybe some stained glass somewhere. A special room just for the youth. A better sound system.

She squeezed her eyes shut. They were burning. The smell was awful.

Mom was crying again.

Elise took her father's hand. "We should go home, Dad. There's nothing we can do here."

"All right," he said. But he didn't move.

She understood.

A car pulled into the lot behind them. Elise turned to see a short man stepping out of one of those cute arrest-me-red sports cars. She didn't know him, or the car, so she said, "Who's that?" to nobody in particular.

Her father let go of her hand and went to the man. "Paul," he said as they shook hands, "I'm glad you're here."

Great, thought Elise. *One more person to stare with us at the heap that used to be our church.*

But Paul didn't stare. He didn't even look. All of

his attention was focused on her father. "Are you all right?" he asked him.

"I don't know what I am right now," her father replied.

"That's understandable."

Silence.

"Listen," Paul said, "you'll rebuild, right? And in the meantime, I'll talk to my board. You'll need a place to meet. Maybe we can work something out. Move service times around."

"I haven't thought about any of that yet," her father admitted. He sounded exhausted.

"Of course you haven't," Paul said. "Sorry."

More silence.

Then the man (Was he another pastor offering to let them use his church building?) said, "Alec, why don't you and your family come over to my house this afternoon? We'll eat. Get our families together." He paused as he wrote his address on a slip of paper and handed it to Elise. "You shouldn't stay here."

Please, Dad, Elise thought, ready to do anything if it meant getting away from this parking lot. She had never seen her father look the way he looked now. Lost, almost. It frightened her. *He's right. You shouldn't stay here.*

* * *

Ed Cooper sat on the couch, watching his son watch him. They'd been sitting there like that all morning and something had to give. "You didn't run today," he said.

"No sir," Will replied.

Had it been Ed's idea for Will to call him *sir*? He couldn't remember. He only knew that Will always had. "Have you been running at all? School starts in a couple weeks. Won't you want to be getting ready for cross country?"

"Haven't felt like running, sir."

Ed knew well enough what Will *had* felt like doing. He'd been doing plenty of it the past few weeks. Drinking. He didn't like what it was doing to Will, but he figured it wasn't his place to tell him not to do it. Ed Cooper might be a lot of bad things, but he was no hypocrite. He laughed. "How come you're not drinking today?"

Will shrugged. "'Cause it's Sunday, I guess." He looked at the carpet at the toe of his boot. "Why aren't you, sir?"

"Pastor Hale got me thinking," he admitted slowly, watching for a reaction from his son. There was none. "I told him I'm no drunk. He said I was. I told him I could quit anytime. He said try it." He paused. "So I'm trying it."

"Why do you care what he thinks?"

Ed noticed that his son hadn't asked the question like he really cared about the answer. His tone was flat. Disrespectful. His eyes were angry. Indignant. And he hadn't said *sir*.

Truth was, Ed didn't care what anybody thought. He had his reasons for drinking, and if people had a problem with it, it was their hard luck. But a man had challenged him. "Turn on the radio, will you?" he said to Will.

Without hesitation Will obeyed.

But after four or five songs, Ed had had enough. After all, he was sober this morning. "Turn it off," he said.

Will reached up to do it...and then stopped. "No."

Ed had never tolerated that response, and Will hadn't tried it in years. Why was he challenging now? About a stupid radio. "Turn it off."

Staring right at him, Will said, "No." Pause. "Sir."

Before Ed became aware enough of what he was doing to think about stopping, he was across the room, holding Will up against the wall and shouting at him. "When I tell you to do something, you do it *NOW!* Do you hear me?" He shook Will. "I said, do you hear..."

Hearing his own words and feeling that all too familiar hatred scared Ed. Really scared him. In the past when he'd bothered to analyze his behavior toward his son, its violence and its unforgiving demanding, he'd attributed it to the fact that he was always drunk when it happened. Out of his control. Wrong, but excusable somehow.

But today he was sober.

And his rage was just as present. Just as potent.

As powerful as the fearful but determined defiance in his son's eyes.

"Will..." Ed released his son's shoulders and stepped away from him.

"What!" Will shouted. "Are you going to hit me? Are you? Well, do it, then. Do it!"

It wasn't that Ed didn't want to hit Will. He did. But now, unlike when he was drunk or simply too intimidated by what Pastor Hale might do if he did, he knew that he shouldn't. He didn't move. His shoulders tensed and his fists went so tight that he could feel his pulse in his fingers, but he refused to hit his son.

Confusion showed in Will's eyes.

"I'm not going to hit you, Will," Ed stiffly said.

Will laughed. "Yes you are."

"No. I'm not."

As Will's expression turned uncertain again, Ed allowed himself to notice how much his son did look like Sarah. The same brown hair. The same eyes. "I'm not going to hit you," he said.

"Yes you are!" Will ran toward him and pushed him back. "You have to! I disobeyed you! You have to!"

After struggling a moment to regain his balance and to guess what could be going on inside his son's mind to make him behave so uncharacteristically and almost desperately, Ed placed his hands on Will's shoulders. With a steady stare and a quiet voice he said, "Will, I'm not going to hit you. What's—?"

"You have to," Will insisted just as quietly. "I disobeyed you. I deserve it. You have to hit me. Don't you get it? I deserve it." Tears had filled Will's eyes, making him look very small to Ed. Like a child instead of the man he'd been only moments ago. "I deserve it."

Ed didn't know what to do. Part of him, a part he'd shoved away for so long that he'd almost forgotten it had existed at all, called to him to hold his son. To comfort him. To forgive him.

Had it really been Will's *fault*? Or—

No! It *had* been his fault. Ed could not forgive his son's disobedience when the smallest moment of it had stolen from him the only thing that had ever mattered.

But Sarah had loved Will. Enough to throw herself in front of a moving truck to protect him. Had she done that just so Will could grow up in the worst kind of unsafeness? No. No.

But...

Slowly, unable to offer his son the forgiveness he needed and unwilling to deliver to him the hatred he apparently thought he wanted and deserved, Ed turned away. "Leave, Will," he said.

"Sir?"

"Get out!"

This time Will obeyed. Without hesitation. Like always.

Ed heard the screen door click shut, the pounding of Will's hurried steps on the porch, and gravel crunching as the pickup sped from the driveway. The confusion inside Ed at that moment paralyzed him. Stung him. He forced himself to stop thinking.

After turning off the radio himself, he walked through the dining room—so much Sarah's—and into the kitchen. He needed a drink.

No.

He needed to talk with Pastor Hale.

But it was Sunday. The man wouldn't have time for him.

It didn't matter.

He looked at the can of beer in his hand, and then at his car keys on the counter. Leaving the beer and grabbing the keys, he ran out the back door and to his car.

Even if he couldn't see Pastor Hale today, he wasn't going to sit at home, get drunk, and hide from this thing. He had spent too many years hiding. Now it was time to do some seeking.

Sarah had not died for it to be this way.

She had loved Will, and would have expected Ed to do the same.

But could he? And, if he could, would Will let him?

* * *

Justin Corelli helped his mother carry the last of the serving bowls to the dining room just as the doorbell rang. Pastor Alec Hale and his family. Justin was looking forward to finally meeting the man his father couldn't seem to say enough good things about, although he would have preferred different circumstances. He hoped to be able to offer the man some sort of encouragement, but felt inadequate for the task. Unlike his father, who frequently moved from church to church, never really feeling as if any of them were truly his because he knew he'd be somewhere else within a couple of years, Pastor Alec Hale had built his church. Pioneered it. Stuck with it through its ups and downs. His church was his. And even though a church consisted of much more than the building, it had to be killing him that his building had been destroyed so completely and unexpectedly. So brutally.

Had the same people or person who had been vandalizing all the other churches attacked Alec Hale's? If so, why had they burned it to the ground when they'd been content just to do damage to the others?

As in all the other cases, police had no leads. They remained as clueless about who was committing these crimes as the rest of the population. Nobody knew anything about the vandals except that they hated Christians. All Christians. Christianity.

Why?

Ironic, Justin thought, *that to its enemies, Christianity is one unit. One religion. A thing to stand against. If only we saw ourselves that way and acted on it instead of allowing ourselves to be distracted by making enemies of one another.* He smiled. *Like father, like son, or what?*

"Justin, let them in, please," Dad said from the back deck. "I'm getting the burgers off the grill."

"Sure, Dad," he called as he hurried to the front door.

* * *

Sickened by what she'd just heard on the radio, Kyra Gress stood and walked slowly downstairs to use the phone in the kitchen. She found Jon Hale's telephone number on her list from the coffeehouse, which she'd taped to the bottom of their church roster, and dialed.

An answering machine.

She hung up without leaving a message. The thing was probably already filled with people expressing horror and grief over what had happened to the Hales' church. Kyra figured that after a certain point those kinds of messages would end up hurting more than helping, and she didn't want to add to it. She'd wait until she could talk to Jon in person.

She'd met Jon only four weeks ago, though of course she'd seen him at school, when she'd first started helping out at the coffeehouse. She couldn't say she liked him, exactly. It was more like he intrigued her. His ideas. He had a confidence in what he believed that she half admired and half resented. And even if he was sometimes egotistical and obstinate and a little off in his doctrine, Kyra respected him.

And now she hurt for him. For his family, especially his father.

What kind of psycho would burn down a church?

Going back up to her room, she prayed that somehow God would comfort the Hales. Assure them of His love. His sovereignty.

* * *

"Alec, what is it?" Stephanie Hale looked with concern at her husband, who was staring at the boy who'd just opened Pastor Corelli's front door. Though she'd been wanting to meet Alec's friend Paul and his family, and though she was certain their invitation today had been extended with the best of intentions, Stephanie did not feel like socializing. She wanted to be home. Alone with Alec. Free to cry if she wanted to, which she did. But Alec had responded with such relief to Paul's suggestion that she hadn't objected. Now, though, he was standing there as if he had been slapped. "Alec?"

Her husband only shook his head.

"I'm Justin," the boy said as he stepped back. "Come in."

"Thank you." Alec waited while Jon and Elise, and then Stephanie, entered. He grinned at Pastor Corelli's son and said, "You're Justin."

"Yes, sir."

Jon said, "He's Justin?"

Suddenly Stephanie understood her husband's strange behavior. The boy's almost disbelieving stare. Had it been a different day, a day when images of their destroyed church building weren't assaulting and distracting her mind, Stephanie might have made the connection sooner.

Justin!

The boy who had been attacked by the wolverine!

The boy her husband had helped.

"I don't believe this," she said, shaking her head. "I don't believe this."

Nobody said anything else until Pastor Corelli walked into the room and introduced himself. He looked at each one of them, his smile turning to a curious frown, and asked, "What'd I miss?"

"Dad," Justin said, "this is the guy that got Corey and me off the mountain."

Pastor Corelli's expression before he said, "You're kidding!" was so comical that Stephanie couldn't hold back a smile. The first one all day.

But not the last.

* * *

By dusk, Will Cooper was ready to talk. To "get real" with his problem. He had already driven to Jon Hale's house, but nobody had been there so he'd decided to see if he could find him at the Hales' church. Jon went there sometimes to practice music.

Will pulled his pickup into the empty parking lot, killed the engine, and sat there, his mouth open, his mind unable to digest what his eyes were telling him.

"Jeez," he whispered after a while. Slowly he stepped down out of his truck and quietly shut the door. The smell of burned wood and grass and the stench of soaked ashes hung thick in the dry air. "What the…?" *Had Jon been inside? Pastor Hale?*

Will ran back to his truck. He'd been thinking all day that maybe he could find some answers in Jon Hale's God. Some peace. But now he knew that there could be no such God. No such peace. He glanced once more at what was left of the Hales' church.

If this was the way God treated people who loved Him, how would He treat Will Cooper?

* * *

Alec and Paul had been walking for nearly two hours when Alec realized where he wanted to go.

They'd decided to walk off the two-too-many hamburgers they'd each eaten, but until now they'd been walking in no particular direction. "I want to go to my church," he said.

He could feel Paul's reluctance before he spoke and then heard it in his question. "Are you sure, Alec?"

"Yeah."

A pause. Then, "Okay."

They walked several blocks without speaking before Alec could bring himself to say what he'd been thinking all day. "Paul," he said, "I feel like God has ripped the safe ground I thought I was standing on right out from under me." When Paul said nothing, Alec went on. "I mean, is He trying to tell me I shouldn't pastor anymore? What?" Frustration tightened his throat. "I don't understand."

"Your building isn't the seal of your pastorate," Paul said quietly. "I know we might come from different perspectives on that because I move around all the time and you don't." He paused. "This was *your* church. I've never felt that way about a building. But, as far as God ripping things away from you, I guess you'd have to weigh that against your doctrine about foreknowledge vs. predestination."

"What do you mean?" Alec asked.

"I mean whatever you believe about God in relation to the things that happen in our lives. Is He *causing* them, *allowing* them, or simply *working with* them? Your take on these questions will determine how you respond to the things that happen."

Alec thought about that. "What do you think?"

"I think someone burned your church down," Paul answered.

Alec waited. "And?"

"And nothing. It rains on the just and the unjust. What concerns God is what you do with it now."

Paul's almost casual attitude, as if they were discussing the theft of the family lawnmower rather than the torching of Alec's whole life, was beginning to offend Alec. But he didn't say so. He said, "Paul, I'm talking real life, here. Not doctrinal principle."

"I know," Paul said more gently. "But that's my point. Doctrine *is* real life. If you believe that God is in control, in charge, directly responsible for everything that happens to you, then you might wonder if He might be trying to rid you of your pastorate. Or you might look at this as His way of getting you out of your comfort zone so He'd be free to move you onto bigger and better things. Or," he added, laughing quietly, "He didn't like your carpet."

Alec had to laugh with his friend. That was ridiculous, of course. But Paul's overall point intrigued him. Had he ever formally pondered what he believed about God's part in the daily lives of His children? He supposed he had on some basic theological level, and he knew that he'd counseled and comforted people with the assurance that God was in control. But now he had to wonder what that meant, exactly, *in control.*

A question for another day, maybe. A day when he wasn't so exhausted. So unsettled.

"Paul," he said, "thanks for being here for me today. I appreciate it."

"You'd do the same for me."

Alec nodded. He would.

"Trials strengthen us," Paul reminded him, not for the first time that day.

Though he knew he should be finding encouragement in knowing that, he wasn't. He felt weak and uncertain. Not about God's love for him. Not because he didn't know that he, his family, and his church would survive this. But inside. In himself. He didn't like when he couldn't see where he was going.

But he forbade himself to surrender to this or any other fear. When he found time to pray about the situation, to think beyond the obvious, it wouldn't look so bad. It had been a surprise attack on his confidence. That was all. He'd handle it. God would handle it.

What was a building, anyway?

A shell for the church. A place to stay protected from the elements.

Nothing, really.

Right?

Right.

So why did it nearly kill him to step onto his parking lot and see that *easily replaced, nothing important* gone? A wrong natural attachment to something he had built? After all, whose church was it? If God wanted it burned down, or even if it was just okay with Him that it was, who was Alec Hale to mind?

No. God did not want this.

But He had allowed it. At the very least, He had allowed it.

Alec stopped walking and shut his eyes. Tired.

Paul's hand on his shoulder. "You okay?"

"I will be," Alec said.

Paul nodded. Then he pointed to the other end of the parking lot. "Someone from your church?"

Alec looked. Will Cooper.

Oh, please, Lord, he prayed silently, *how can I give him anything tonight when I feel so drained?*

As always, God's persistent reminder: *You can't, but I can.*

"He's a friend of Jon's," Alec told Paul as they walked toward Will, who was holding onto his driver's side door as if he was just about to pull it open.

"Pastor Hale," Will said, lowering his hand to his side. "I was looking for Jon." He briefly scanned the pile of debris in front of them and then looked questioningly up at Alec. "Are you all all right?"

"Yes." He related what he knew about the fire, assured Will that nobody had been inside the building when it had happened, introduced him to Paul, and then asked, "How are things, Will? With your father."

"I don't want to talk about him, sir," Will said. "I had some questions about God." He shrugged. "I was looking to talk about God."

And that's exactly what the three of them did. For the next hour and a half. Sitting on the gravel beside Will's truck, right in front of Pastor Alec Hale's burned down church. As they spoke, it suddenly ceased mattering to Alec that he was a pastor without a building, or that the Christian beside him, who was doing most of the talking tonight, interpreted I

Corinthians 13:9-13 differently than he did.

All that mattered was the boy in front of him. His brokenness.

And his surrender.

6

"I'm sorry. I've made my position clear."

Molly Avery stared at Pastor Corelli, angry. No, furious. Not only was he refusing to perform the wedding ceremony for her wedding to Kent next month, but he'd just told her that he'd also decided not to let them use the building. It went against everything he stood for, he'd said.

Well, Molly Avery didn't care what Paul Corelli stood for.

This was her church.

She couldn't understand, even though he had explained it twice, why he would not let them use the building. So what if Kent wasn't a Christian? Molly had heard the most recent church gossip. People had been whispering for two weeks now about Pastor Corelli asking the board to consider making their building available after their Sunday service to the congregation whose building had been burned down. A charismatic congregation, Molly had heard. Though she genuinely felt sorry for those people and hoped the board would agree to share their facility with them until other arrangements could be made, Molly had to wonder about her pastor's reasoning.

Why was it okay to let two hundred charismatic people into their sanctuary every Sunday morning to do God knew what with snakes, tambourines, and aerobic worship when it wasn't okay to let Molly Avery, a member of the church for twenty-six years, use it for two hours on a Friday night for her wedding?

She looked straight at her pastor and asked, "Don't you think you're being unnecessarily legalistic?"

Pastor Corelli leaned forward to meet her stare. "Why is it considered wrong now to see standards in the Word and try to live by them? Legalism has turned into a bad word, but it isn't always such a bad thing."

"What about our testimony to Kent?" she shot at him. "How will this demonstrate the love of Christ to him?"

Without even the slightest hesitation, Pastor Corelli said, "It's by showing him a watered-down gospel which he can take or leave depending on whether or not it's convenient at any given time that we do him the disservice, Molly." He paused and then asked, "Why do you care about having a church wedding?"

"Because I've always wanted one," she snapped, and regretted the answer immediately. It sounded so...unspiritual.

"Why?" he pressed.

The answer she would have given just a few months ago—*Because I want to dedicate my marriage to God*—seemed somehow not applicable to her situation with Kent, so she said nothing.

"Have you ever shared the gospel with Kent?"

"Yes."

"And?"

"He's not interested," she said. What she didn't say was how Kent laughed at her whenever she tried to discuss Jesus and her relationship with Him. Or that he'd always say, *"Why would I want to become a Christian, Molly? So I can feel guilty, too, about what we're doing? No thanks!"* Molly looked away from Pastor Corelli at the engagement ring on her finger as her hand went to a fist in her lap.

"Molly," Pastor Corelli said gently, "this isn't about me or my standards, or even this church building. This is about you and your commitment to Christ. I have no doubt that you love Kent and that you believe that God will eventually work all things together for your good by bringing Kent to Himself through you. And maybe He will. But why take the hard road? Scripture is clear about marrying unbelievers, Molly. A lot more clear than it is about a lot of other things. Things that people have died to defend."

Strange. Her comeback about the different cultural influences of the early church seemed to hold less potential now in Pastor Corelli's office than it had during the past few weeks when she'd relied on it late at night. But still, she loved Kent, and she was going to marry him. Nothing the man in front of her could say or do would change that.

She stood quickly and said, "You are a self-righteous, unreasonable man. I can find plenty of other pastors who'll marry us and let us use their church!"

"Yes. You can do that."

"I suppose you think you're better than they are?"

"This isn't about me, Molly," Pastor Corelli replied quietly, not even flinching at her rage.

She turned to leave his office, mumbling, "Oh, yes it is."

* * *

Considering the way Kyra insisted that she no longer had a crush on Justin Corelli, Corey Gress expected her to find someone else to eat lunch with now that the first few days of school were over and the school cafeteria held no shortage of his sister's friends. But there she was again, sitting beside Justin. Oh well. Corey really didn't mind. For a little sister, Kyra was acceptable company, and her random interjections into a conversation always kept things lively.

"So," she was asking as Corey sat down and reached for his cheeseburger, "what do you guys think?"

Corey bit into his sandwich. "About?"

"About sharing our church with Pastor Hale's church?"

Though he knew they owed a lot to Pastor Hale because he'd helped Justin, Corey had his doubts about the arrangement Pastor Corelli had presented to their church board. But he wanted to get a feel for everyone else's opinion before stating his. "What do you think?" he asked his sister.

She grinned. "Coward!" Then her face went serious. "I think it's cool."

"What if it wasn't Pastor Hale's church?" Corey pressed. "What if it was just some other charismatic church?"

"I don't think my dad would do it if he didn't know the pastor," Justin said. "But he and Pastor Hale have been praying together for a long time."

Kyra glared at Corey, and spoke to Justin. "He means, what if Pastor Hale hadn't saved your life?"

"Well," Corey said defensively, "it's not like it's not a valid question. Is Pastor Corelli giving this guy a mile where he'd otherwise only give half because he figures he owes him, or something?"

"Corey," Justin answered, "my dad told Pastor Hale he'd talk to our board before he even knew it was him who helped me. He did it because they're friends. Because the guy's church is gone." He paused. "I'd hope that someone would help us out if those creeps ever burned down our building."

"So you think it's a good idea?" Corey asked Justin directly. Justin always defended his father first even if he was still working through some thoughts of his own.

"In theory," he said, "yeah. But I'd be lying if I didn't admit that it makes me a little nervous. When we were in New York I went on a youth retreat with some friends of mine from one of those big, loud,

My-diamond-rings-are-the-proofs-of-my-calling type churches. I went mostly because I was curious. My friend Tim, who went to church there, prayed for me once when I had a really bad flu. And I'm not kidding. I did get healed. I mean, it was gone. Just like that. At the moment he prayed. And it didn't come back later when the 'hype' had worn off. So I was curious. Maybe there was something to all this healing stuff."

"Your father let you go?" Kyra asked, surprised.

Justin nodded. "He's always had this thing about unity. He said I could go as long as I talked with him about any questions I had when I got back."

"Did you have any questions?" Corey asked.

Justin nodded. "More than one. But the biggest thing was that once Tim told everyone that I didn't pray in tongues, they wouldn't leave me alone about it. Then one afternoon after chapel, they all kind of closed in around me, acting like they wouldn't let me leave until I received my supposed tongue."

"Did you?" Kyra asked.

"No! Be serious!"

"I was," she said.

"I don't believe in that. I don't care if they lock me in a closet and deprive me of food and water."

"I was just asking," Kyra insisted. "Peer pressure can do a lot."

"Yeah," Justin said. "Well, after that they weren't my peers anymore. It was scary. They all had their hands on me, telling me to 'let it go' and 'let God give you the words' and all that. Some of them were praying in tongues the whole time except when they shouted 'Jesussss!' at me." He shook his head. "Too weird."

"Well, if it's any consolation," Kyra said, "I know Pastor Hale's son and he's not anything like that."

"I know," said Justin.

"How do you know his son?" Corey asked Kyra.

"From the coffeehouse."

"Oh." Corey had never visited the place. Mostly because he preferred to be spending his Friday and Saturday evenings driving home after a day of fishing.

"Hey," Kyra said, pointing toward the cafeteria doors, "there's Jon Hale with Shayna Quinn and Will Cooper." She stood. "I'm going to invite them to come eat with us." Before she left, though, she leaned toward Justin and said, "Will is the kid your dad and Pastor Hale led to the Lord the day their church burned down. He's a totally different person now."

"She knows everyone," Justin said, laughing.

Corey nodded. "Me? I'm happy at a lake by myself."

After Kyra returned and introduced everyone who needed to be introduced, the conversation moved quickly and excitedly from class schedules, to cross country, to the coffeehouse, and then to their two churches.

How would it work, sharing the building?

Would their youth groups do things together?

Would they ever attempt a joint service?

Would the board of Pastor Corelli's church even approve the idea?

"Why wouldn't they?" Will Cooper asked Jon

Hale. His first comment of the conversation.

Jon leaned forward, clearly unsure of the best way to answer.

Shayna wrote an *S* in her ketchup with the tip of a french fry.

"I mean," Will went on, "we're all Christians, right? What's the big deal?"

"Oh, you know," Kyra said quickly, nervously, "service times and all."

That seemed to satisfy Will Cooper and the conversation shifted—not completely smoothly, but easily enough—to the horrors of cafeteria dining.

Corey, for one, was relieved. He did not want to be part of breaking it to such a new believer that all was not perfect or simple inside the faith he'd just embraced.

* * *

After a brief prayer and a long recounting of old business, Bruce Finch opened the floor to the only topic the board was interested in discussing, anyway: Should they grant Pastor Corelli the freedom to open the church facility for the congregation whose church had been burned down?

"I think we should," said one board member immediately. "I don't even see why we have to discuss it. Those people have a need that we can meet without too much inconvenience."

"I don't think anyone's debating that point," said another man.

"We haven't officially debated anything yet,"

Bruce Finch reminded his colleagues. "Entryway politics aren't part of the official process."

"So you'll have to say it for the record," the first board member who had spoken said coldly to the second. "What point are we debating?"

"Let's not play games," said a third man. Then he turned to Bruce. "Some of us have some concerns about the doctrine of Pastor Hale's congregation. And…" He looked down at the blank notepad on the table in front of him. "And about Pastor Corelli's motives for bringing this up in the first place."

"What concerns?" Bruce asked, though he already knew because he shared them. Most of them.

"I say we vote now," someone said. "We all know how we feel already, and talking about it isn't going to change any of our minds. It's either going to be yes or no. Why waste time in a conversation that's only going to upset people?"

Ordinarily, Bruce wouldn't consider the option of voting without discussion. But this case was different. "I think Rick's right," he said.

A couple of men muttered disagreement, but most around the table appeared to be relieved.

"Those in favor of opening our facility to Pastor Hale's church until December 1rst?"

Five men raised their hands.

Bruce Finch grimaced. Unless one of the other five board members declined to vote, he'd have to break the tie. "Those opposed?"

All five men remaining raised their hands.

In response to the ten tense stares in his direction, Bruce grinned and said, "I guess it's up to me."

* * *

During Cross Country training after school, Jon Hale and Will Cooper ran side by side well ahead of everyone else on the team. Jon could feel the beginning pangs of one of his all too frequent sideaches, though, and slowed down.

So did Will. "Jon?"

"Yeah?"

"You know how we were talking about your churches today at lunch?"

Jon nodded.

"I guess I've never thought about it before, but, why are there so many different Christian churches?"

"Whew," Jon said. "What a question!"

Will waited.

"Different interpretations of certain passages of the Bible, mostly," Jon said.

"But they're all Christians, right?"

Jon opted for the easy answer. "If a person has acknowledged that he's sinful where God isn't, and that there's no way he can earn or work or hope his way into eternity with God except because of Jesus' death on the cross and His resurrection, then he's a Christian. If he hasn't acknowledged that, and if he hasn't committed his life to Christ, then he's not. Every so-named Christian church probably has people in both situations."

"Yeah," Will said, "so how does a person decide where to go to church?"

"That's where the different interpretations of the

Bible come in. I think most "Christian" churches agree about how we are saved, but not all. Beyond that, though…" He laughed.

"What?"

"Well, just to give you an idea of the hugeness of the question you're asking…" Jon took a deep breath. Talking while running was not helping his sideache. He said, "Some churches believe we have to be baptized in a full tank of water. Some think it's okay to just get sprinkled. Some churches baptize babies, and some wait until the person has made a commitment to Christ at whatever age and don't baptize before then. Some people think we need to be baptized in the name of Jesus Christ. Some people say you have to say all three names—the Father, the Son, and the Holy Spirit. Some people think you have to be baptized in order to be saved. Some people don't. Some people think you automatically receive the Holy Spirit when you're baptized in water. Some people think the baptism of the Holy Spirit is an entirely different and separate thing. Some people…"

"Whoa," said Will. "I get the picture."

Relieved, Jon said, "And that's just baptism!"

"I guess I'll have to start reading the Bible," Will said, and then mentioned the race coming up in a couple of weeks.

Because he had no doubt that their conversation could have become a lot more complicated than it had, Jon did not reroute it back when Will finished talking about the new shoes he was planning to buy. He stayed silent, grateful for the opportunity to repace his breathing.

* * *

Stephanie and Elise Hale sat at their dining room table cutting fresh vegetables for tonight's fajitas, waiting for Alec to come home with news about Pastor Corelli's board's decision. As much as Stephanie liked Paul and Rose Corelli, she couldn't quite get comfortable with the idea of sharing their church building.

Hers wasn't a doctrinal difficulty, though the two churches obviously disagreed about many significant things. Nor was she concerned with the logistics of two churches sharing one building. They'd work it out, she was sure. How complicated could it be?

It was the matter of being the one in need that troubled Stephanie Hale. She had been a pastor's daughter and then a pastor's wife. Always giving. Always providing comfort and answers. Always having everything together. Or at least that was the expectation. And in the case of her father, and then Alec, there had never been much difficulty in living up to that expectation.

Until now.

Stephanie Hale was realizing with every thought of using a building that other people had labored to build and maintain, that she didn't know how to receive. She felt guilty. Like a sponge.

Like she and Alec must have failed, somehow.

Knowing that she wouldn't feel superior in any way to Paul Corelli and his church if the situation were reversed did little to appease her apprehension.

But she knew it should. And she knew human

pride when she felt it twist in her stomach. It was wrong to feel the way she was feeling. She knew that. And yet the feelings persisted.

Clearly, this was one of those situations which God would use to further refine her. It was uncomfortable. It was unfamiliar. But Stephanie Hale was not afraid of God's refining.

She'd just have to trust Him.

And her husband.

* * *

"Thanks, Bruce." Paul Corelli shook the Church Board President's hand and watched him until he turned the corner after the sanctuary doors. Then he walked slowly into his office and closed the door.

He nodded at Alec, who was standing near the window. *Good news or bad news, buddy. Which do you want first?* He decided to give it to him all at once. "It was a close vote," he said, "but you're in."

Alec stayed at the window. "How close?"

Paul hesitated. "Six—five."

"Too close," Alec said. "I'm not willing to be the cause of a strain between you and your board, Paul. It's been working out all right, meeting in homes."

Paul laughed. "It's obvious you've never had a board." He sat on the edge of his desk. "No reason is needed for strife. It's just part of the territory."

"Maybe so, but…"

"Alec, Alec," he said, shaking his head and putting the New York accent on as thick as he could, "I don' like 'no', an' I don' heah 'no'. So don' say it."

Serious again, he said, "You need a building. We have a building. We'll just have to prove to them that this can work."

For several moments, Alec stared at the cloud-less sky outside Paul's window without speaking. Finally, quietly, he said, "What if it doesn't?"

"Then," Paul said, standing to join his friend at the window, "yer out on yuh caaan!"

Both men laughed and then sat down on opposite sides of Paul's desk to work at a schedule that would accommodate both congregations.

7

S unday morning two weeks later, Paul returned to his office after service, impressed that most of his congregation had remembered to come an hour earlier than usual and that they'd seemed happy to do it. He'd expressed his appreciation from the pulpit at the end of his sermon just before reminding them to fellowship downstairs so that Pastor Hale's people could get right in to the sanctuary and start their service on time.

Nobody mentioned the inconvenience, although Paul had noticed strained expressions on two or three faces.

They'll get used to it.

Personally, Paul preferred an earlier start and finish to Sunday services. More family time. Lunch before 1:00.

And Alec's people? They could sleep in. Enjoy a big breakfast before church. They had definitely received the more difficult end of the arrangement, but Paul had already received several calls and cards thanking him and his congregation for their willingness to put themselves out by sharing their building.

Peoples' attitudes would either uphold or defeat this endeavor.

Time would tell.

This morning, Paul was hopeful. Confident, even.

He lingered in his office awhile, filing his sermon notes and putting the tithe checks received today in an envelope for the secretary to sort and record in the morning. Whenever he looked up and saw people passing by his window on their way to the church's main entrance for Alec's service, Paul couldn't deny a certain amount of curiosity about them. Who were they? What was their average age? Their average education? Their average income? What had drawn them to a local church with no affiliation to any religious organization rather than to—and often out of—one with the heritage and permanence of a traditional denomination? He noticed that they were dressed only slightly more casually than the people in his own congregation. That the children seemed just as well behaved. That many of the teenagers were as visibly bored about arriving at church as was generally the case before his own services.

Through the window, Alec's people looked a lot like his own.

Paul smiled. Had he really expected them to look otherwise? Dressed in torn jeans and contemporary Christian T-shirts, maybe? Or overdressed, with diamond jewelry visible on every neck, ear, wrist, and finger? Had he expected the children to be more unruly, perhaps? Less respectful? Maybe a little. And hadn't he expected the teens to be somewhat more excited about church, since a 'Spirit-filled' service was supposed to be so much more relevant than a traditional one?

Even though he knew Alec and had no doubts about his integrity, his genuineness, and his ability to pastor, Paul realized to his own shame that he'd surrendered without much of a fight to so many stereotypes of the 'average' charismatic congregation.

"Hmm," he muttered to himself as he turned away from the window to stare instead at his family picture on the bookshelf. *And you know that that kind of unconscious prejudice is aimed at you, too, pal.*

Socially advanced, spiritually asleep.

A congregation made up of cute older couples who knew every word to every verse of "Crown Him With Many Crowns" and the books of the Bible in order but couldn't pray their way out of a paper bag.

Legalistic. Boring. Cemetery—oops, I meant Seminary—doctrine.

Services to sleep through.

Dead religion.

Paul stood, flipped the light switch off, stepped out into the hall, and pulled his office door shut. As he walked toward the back stairway to head downstairs to find Rose, Jessica, and Justin, he heard something he'd never before heard inside a church building.

A very loud 'lick' on a bass guitar.

He smiled. The one stereotype of charismatic churches that he'd failed to think of. *People jumping up and down with hands raised and tears in their eyes while dancing with one another's spouses and rapping the Nicene Creed.*

Paul stopped to have a listen, definitely hoping that this was another stereotype that Alec's church would fail to live up to. Or down to.

And it was.

Though loud, and with a clear appeal to a younger generation, the music which filled Paul's sanctuary for nearly thirty minutes intrigued him as did its apparent effect on Alec's people and on himself. Paul believed that sacred music should be sacred in its musical structure as well as in its words. He believed that the contemporary attempt to use the vehicle of rock music to convey Christ's message would fail because the world would see no difference between itself and that which was meant to be sacred even when you *could* understand the words. So far, the lifestyles of too many contemporary Christian musicians had all too adequately borne this out. Though he didn't necessarily buy all the teaching he'd heard about certain rock beats and Satan, Paul didn't figure you'd need much spiritual discernment to see Satan's ugly fingerprints all over the secular music scene. Drugs. Sex. Violent lyrics. Rebellion. Anti-women. Anti-authority. Anti-God.

The church should be different.

Truly different.

Not just a Christianized version of the world.

And yet...

We have Christian television, don't we? That's contemporary. A medium of the secular world. Don't we utilize magazines? Radio? We have Christian apparel. Christian jewelry. Christian book clubs, CD clubs, computer software clubs. We even have Christian fiction, for heaven's sake!

What's so different about music?

Paul had to wonder.

There might not be a difference, he thought, *if people could just learn to separate the music from the lifestyles of its secular counterparts. Do I want Justin wearing clothes that are ten sizes too big for him and 'moshing' to some upbeat version of "Jesus Loves the Little Children"? I don't think so. Or Jessica. Would I be content to watch her moan and groan seductively into a microphone because the love song she was singing had been written for Jesus? I don't think so.*

But can we really expect a choir singing hymns to truly reach or impact today's youth?

Paul didn't know.

What he did know was that the passion, the reverence, and the power of all that contemporary sounding praise music coming from his sanctuary had stilled him. One of the last things he would have expected from anything having to do with a charismatic service was stillness. But there he stood. Stilled. Awed. Listening to people he didn't know—Christians he didn't know—worship.

"Lord, free our hearts to worship
as we near the gates of praise.
In expectant awe, we seek Your presence,
and treasure the glory in this place.

In this place...in this place
my soul is fully open to the power of Your grace.
In this place...in this place
our God is in this place.
Our God is in this place."

And:

"Lord, I want my life to glorify Your name,
Every word and deed in some way to proclaim
Your unfailing love,
Your mercy and Your truth,
Lord, I want my life to bring honor to You."

Paul stopped thinking about the yeas and nays of the issue of contemporary Christian music. He stopped thinking about the fact that the two hundred people on the other side of the wall behind him believed that they could legitimately prophecy right here and now. He stopped thinking about what his board members would say if they were still here and could hear this music from downstairs.

He was thinking about God.

* * *

Ed Cooper glanced for the third time at the clock on the wall above the stove. Nearly noon. Will had left an hour ago to meet his friends for breakfast before heading to church.

Who'd ever heard of such a thing? Starting church at noon.

Ed stirred his coffee.

"You should come sometime," Pastor Hale had suggested at the end of their most recent counseling meeting.

"I sleep in on the weekends," Ed had absently replied.

Pastor Hale had laughed. "Well I guess you'll be up by noon." And he'd left it at that.

Actually, Ed had been up by 6:00. Probably because he hadn't been drinking last night. In fact, he hadn't taken a drink in weeks.

"A lot of good it's doing me," he muttered.

Tension between him and Will seemed to have intensified rather than lessened. But maybe it only felt that way because he was more aware now. Maybe it had been as suffocating all along.

No. It had gotten worse. Definitely worse. Now that Will knew the details of Sarah's death, he'd barely spoken to Ed. Not that they'd ever really spoken, anyway.

Ed pushed his coffee to the center of the table and lowered his head to his hands.

I can't live like this.

The way Ed Cooper began to see it, he had three choices.

He could continue as he was. Not drinking. Thinking. Trapped in the despair of the 'life' he'd created for himself and Will.

He could go buy a six-pack and try to forget about it for a while.

He could try to find a way to move forward.

"Option number one is definitely out." He stood,

pushed his chair in, took his coffee cup to the sink, and grabbed his car keys.

Where he was going…he wasn't sure yet.

* * *

When the last chorus ended, Stephanie Hale squeezed her husband's hand and then let it go as he walked toward the pulpit and she sat down. On a pew, she couldn't help noticing. Wood. Oak, maybe. Polished to a flawless shine. Hard and uncomfortable, though no more so than the folding metal chairs they had always used at their church.

Alec spoke.

Stephanie paid attention but her eyes were drawn to the things around and behind him. Candles. Two stained glass windows. A purple and gold banner. Fake greenery. Kneelers.

In contrast, their church had always been plain. Deliberately so. It wasn't the ornateness or the 'sacred-lookingness' of a facility that made it a church. And all that stuff cost money. Money that could certainly be put to better, more practical use.

And yet the scenes depicted in the stained glass—Jesus walking on the water, Jesus feeding the multitudes—stirred her. There was something about the cathedral ceilings, the symbolism evident in the items used to distribute the Lord's supper and even in the way they'd been arranged on the table against the back wall, the old organ. All of it, the whole feel of the place…it was *church*. It couldn't just as easily be a hotel conference room.

She smiled. That's what her sister had said about their church the first time she'd visited. "Your sanctuary doesn't look like a church. It looks like a hotel conference room."

Stephanie had, of course, dismissed the comment. It doesn't matter what a church looks like. What matters is what it *is*. What it *does*. What it stands for. That it's warm and dry and clean.

And she still believed that.

Sure, they could have put stained glass windows in their church. But they didn't have the denominational budget. They'd bought children's church materials, toys for the nursery, a sound system. Things that would be used. Useful. They hadn't had money for the decorative and probably wouldn't have spent it that way even if they had.

And maybe they had enjoyed a little pride about that. A small feeling of self righteousness. They were practical Christians into practical Christianity, after all. Who needed stained glass? When did a window ever lead someone to Christ?

Stephanie repented.

There was nothing so horrible about being in a church that looked like a church. In fact, there was a strange serenity about it.

* * *

"That was a great sermon." Shayna Quinn stood between Jon Hale and Will Cooper in the aisle near the front row where they had been sitting. It was 2:00, and even though she'd eaten a late breakfast, she was hungry. "Do you guys want to do something for lunch?"

Jon nodded immediately, but Will acted as if he hadn't even heard the question.

"Hey." Jon elbowed his friend. "You hungry?"

"Nah."

"What's up?" Jon asked him.

Will shrugged. "I guess I'd never thought about the things your dad was talking about today, is all. And I guess I haven't been doing all that great of a job at it."

As Jon tried to explain to Will that you don't just miraculously become The Perfect Christian the moment you accept Christ as your savior, Shayna thought again about Pastor Hale's comments.

Almost any Christian, when asked if he would give his life for Jesus, would certainly say *yes*. They'd take the bullet, the beating, whatever. The one moment of martyrdom. Shayna knew that she would. If someone offered her the choice of denying Christ or dying, she'd choose death. But what did it mean to *die daily* as the scriptures said? That had been Pastor Hale's question. If one would choose to physically die for Christ at any moment, why would he not choose to symbolically die for Him at every other moment? Not tell that lie. Not watch garbage on TV. Not be too afraid to share the gospel with the lady across the street. Not neglect to go to church on Super Bowl Sunday or opening day of hunting season or because you just felt like staying in bed.

Everything we do or don't do, every choice we make or don't make, every attitude we allow ourselves to hold on to...all of it is a reflection of our willingness to live for, and, in some cases, die daily for, Christ.

Shayna had to admit that she didn't have a perfect record in that department, either.

Pastor Hale had read scriptures about the struggle between our fleshly nature and the Spirit. He'd read the scriptures in James about how sin comes to fruition in our lives. He'd read the scriptures about running—living—in such a way as to win the prize.

And then he'd closed the sermon. With a challenge. *Don't go home and beat yourself up over all the ways you've failed this. We all fail this. Christ knows this, and is faithful to forgive us. The goal is to fail less and less. To live and die for Him more and more.*

To think more about the choices we make from now on.

"Little by little, Will," Jon was saying, "He gets rid of the garbage in our lives. As long as you're looking to serve Him, He'll be faithful to finish what He's begun in you."

"I understand that," Will said. "But, okay, let's just get real here. Jesus would want me to forgive my father. Wouldn't you say that?"

Slowly, Jon nodded.

"He'd want me to forgive myself for running out in the street. He'd—"

"Will—"

"Don't interrupt me, Jon."

Shayna watched the two boys' eyes as their wills collided silently for a moment. She wondered what

Will had meant about running out in the street. Jon clearly knew. He told Will to go on.

"He'd want me to, when I'm sitting at the breakfast table with the man…" Will waved his hand like he was shooing away a bug that had irritated him for far too long. "He'd want me to represent Himself to my father."

"Yeah," Jon said. "I'd say that. But—"

"I can't do that."

"Maybe you can't now," Jon said. "But—"

Will shook his head. "I can't do that."

"Come on, man," Jon said. "Don't you really mean you won't?"

Shayna glared at Jon. What an insensitive and self-righteous thing to say. Jon had never in his life had to deal with anything close to the feelings that Will was dealing with now. But Shayna had. Once. She placed her hands on Will's arms and turned him to look at her. "Will, you know what? You're right. You probably can't forgive him. Not by yourself, I mean. But you have to make the first step. You can say, 'Lord, I know You want me to forgive this person. I know You do. I don't see how it's going to happen. Please help me do it.'" She released Will's arms. "And you know what? He will."

Will thought about that for a long moment. He stared so intently at Shayna, through her, really, that she had to look away from him.

Finally, though, he said, "I could do that."

"I'll pray for you," Shayna promised.

Will nodded and then turned back to Jon. "So, are we going for lunch?"

"Sure. Will…"

"Forget it," Will said. "I know what you meant."

The three of them turned and started walking toward the back of the church. Suddenly Will stopped. He was looking at the doors. At one man who was standing there with one foot inside the church and the other on the cement outside. The man stared back at Will. Glared, really, it seemed to Shayna. Then, after a couple of seconds, he left.

Shayna looked curiously at Will. "Was that—?"

"Yeah," Will said. "That was my father."

"He didn't look very happy," Jon observed.

Will shoved his hands in his pockets, and Shayna noticed his whole body, and especially his expression, stiffen as he stood there. "He doesn't know the meaning of the word."

* * *

Vern knew that, at that moment, nobody in the world could be happier than he. It was a gorgeous Sunday afternoon. He was sitting on a stump beside a cooler full of pop, cookies, sandwiches, and carrot sticks, and nobody else was around. The lake was his.

He took his hand off his reel to wave his baseball cap through the mosquitoes swarming around his head.

"Go find another buffet," he muttered.

Even at that, he had to smile.

The day was perfect.

Except for one thing. He couldn't quit thinking about God. Well, not God, exactly. About church and his two pastor friends. Vern didn't like thinking about God because it was one thing he couldn't predict. If he started thinking about racism, say, or abortion or politics or gun control, he knew with a certainty where his thoughts would lead and that his previously drawn conclusions would hold up. He never knew that when he started thinking about God. Yes, he'd drawn conclusions—hadn't everyone?—but the whole issue remained elusive to him. It just wasn't like environmentalism. A guy could know for a fact whether or not cow farts ate away at the ozone layer and state his opinion accordingly. But a guy really couldn't know for a fact whether there was or wasn't a God, or what His name was, or what He expected or wanted.

Could he?

Vern didn't think so. And he'd never seen anything to shake up that thinking.

Until Alec Hale's church had burned down.

He didn't know a lot about what his two pastor friends believed, but he assumed, because they pastored different churches, that they didn't agree about everything. And yet, here they were, sharing Paul Corelli's building. Making it work.

True, they weren't having church together at the same time, but it said a lot about both men and the people they pastored that such a thing could work considering how strongly people tended to feel about the unique rightness of their religion above all others.

He smiled as he bit into a large stalk of celery sticky with too much peanut butter. He had introduced the two pastors and now they were doing something that really mattered together, at least to Vern's way of thinking.

And he couldn't help feeling a certain amount of pride about it, either.

8

As soon as Alec sat beside Paul in the sanctuary Friday morning, he could tell that something was bothering him. But he could also tell, because of the way Paul hurried into his list of prayer requests for the week and then said, "Shall we get to it?" that he didn't want to discuss it.

So the two men prayed. But it remained strained.

"What's up, Paul?" Alec asked after he'd said amen.

Paul smiled, suddenly looking more nervous than troubled. He sighed, leaned heavily back in the pew, and said, "Some of my board members were upset about…"

Alec stiffened. He didn't want the presence of his congregation in their building to put any rifts between Paul and his board, no matter what Paul had said about the inevitability of pastor/board conflict. "Please just tell me, Paul," he said. "I'll take care of it. It's…"

"The way your musicians left the altar after your service last Sunday."

Alec didn't understand.

"The placement of things is important, Alec," Paul explained.

"What things?" He still had no idea what his friend was talking about.

"The candles and…"

Alec let out a shaky breath and shook his head. "Don't do that, Paul," he said. "I thought we really had a problem."

Paul turned to look at him, and he seemed to be trying hard not to glare.

"You're serious." Alec looked up at the pulpit in front of them. "I'm sorry." He stood up, climbed the steps to the platform, scanned the arrangement of the *altar* paraphernalia, and then looked back at Paul. "How about you come show me where stuff is supposed to go? I'm sure my worship leader just didn't realize that it was significant because—well, because we don't have anything on the platform but the pulpit and our instruments. I'll let him know and it won't happen again."

"All right," Paul said, visibly relieved. He joined Alec on the platform to show him where things were supposed to go and to explain the reasoning behind it. When he'd finished, he said, "I was hoping to not have to be discussing issues already. I think maybe my board is looking for them. It wasn't that big a deal to reset things ourselves. To be honest, I'm a little embarrassed to be standing here mentioning it. I'm sorry."

Alec placed his hand firmly on Paul's shoulder. "I'll talk to my worship leader. It won't happen again."

Paul nodded. "That should do it."

But Alec had to wonder if it would.

* * *

Molly Avery accepted the cup of steaming coffee from Raylene Finch and leaned back in her chair to sip it.

"So how are the wedding plans coming?" Raylene asked her. She sat across the table from Molly and straightened the runner with steady fingers.

"You really do have a lovely house," Molly remarked, looking first at the table runner and then at some of the other seemingly little things her hostess had placed here and there around the dining room. Charming. She knew that as a board member's wife, Raylene was expected to do a lot of entertaining. She wondered if Raylene enjoyed it. She knew that she wouldn't. "They're coming along all right, I guess," she said.

"Have you and Kent chosen the place yet?" Raylene asked without looking directly at Molly. Apparently, she felt uncomfortable about the conflict that had arisen between Molly and Pastor Corelli, though not uncomfortable enough to avoid mentioning it.

"Not yet. I just can't believe I won't be having my wedding at the church."

"I'm sure it is upsetting to you." Raylene reached across the table to lightly clasp Molly's hand.

"Do you think he's right?" Molly asked. She hoped the question sounded more grieved than angry, even though she still felt more angry than grieved.

Raylene smiled gently but said nothing.

"I'm sorry," Molly said. "I shouldn't be putting you in that position." She paused. "I guess you have to support him."

Raylene laughed. "Is that what you think the board's job is?"

"Well, yeah. I guess."

"Oh, honey," Raylene said. "Where have you been?"

Now Molly laughed too. "What do you mean?"

"I mean," she said, "that we're only supposed to support him when we don't think he's wrong. That's part of our job. Bruce's job, I mean. To balance the pastor. To keep him accountable. It's just that we're not supposed to talk about it if we think he's wrong."

Molly nodded. She understood. She raised her cup to her lips in an effort to hide the beginning of a smile.

* * *

"Can I sit with you?" Justin Corelli asked his sister Jessica. Normally, he wouldn't have asked, but Jessica had been unusually moody lately and he didn't want to instigate an unpleasant lunch for himself. There were plenty of other tables in the cafeteria.

She shrugged and pushed at her burrito with her fork.

He placed his tray on the table beside hers and

sat down. "What's wrong?"

She sighed. Dramatically. "Cole Simmons has been bugging me again, Justin. 'I hear you're sharing your church with a bunch of snake charmers.'" She pressed her fingers to her temples. "He's such a pain."

Justin laughed. "Pastor Hale is not a snake charmer."

"I know that," she snapped. "He's nice."

"So what's the problem?"

"Cole," she said simply. "He's always harassing me."

"He likes you," Justin teased.

She punched him hard in the arm. "That," she said, "and Dad doesn't want me to try out for the next play at the community theater because he didn't like the script."

Justin nodded. Their father could be very strict about things like that. "Well," he said carefully, "did you think the script was okay?"

She didn't answer.

He grinned. "Well, then, you shouldn't want you to do it, either."

"But I do want to do it, Justin," she said quietly, nearly crying. "I don't know why I have to live his religion even when I don't feel like it just…"

"Because God deserves us to," he said gently.

"Just because he's a pastor," she said as if she hadn't even heard him. "But I don't know why I'm talking about this with you. You've never minded being his puppet. His little show-off piece."

"That's not fair, Jessica." Justin stood and grabbed his tray. His friends had just come into the cafeteria and he'd much rather eat with them. "Enjoy your lunch."

He walked around several tables and across the open floor to where Jon Hale, Will Cooper, Kyra and Corey Gress, and Shayna Quinn were standing, getting condiments.

"Hey, Justin," Corey said. "Come sit with us."

He nodded.

"You okay?" Corey asked.

"Sure," Justin said. "Just glad it's Friday."

"Coffeehouse night," Jon said. "Why don't you come, Corelli?"

"I might have to do that," Justin said, anxious to rid his mind of the things his sister had said to him. "Dad already said I could."

"Well, I'd hope so," Jon said, grinning.

"I guess it would be a little hypocritical of him to pray with your dad and then not let me hang out with you guys, huh?"

Jon looked uncertainly at Justin, as if he couldn't determine whether or not any insult had been intended in his remark. Finally, though, he said, "I guess it would be."

The six of them found a table and sat around it. They began to eat as soon as Jon finished asking the blessing.

Justin stared across the table at Jon Hale. He liked him well enough, and even envied him a little. He seemed so confident in his commitment to God. So at ease with it. Justin loved God, but there was very little ease about his walk with Him. Everything seemed to be a struggle. A forcing of his will. He always wanted to do the right thing, and usually did do it, but it didn't seem to come as readily on the inside as it probably appeared to people watching. He wondered if Jon Hale had to fight so hard. It didn't appear that he did. But didn't his own life prove that appearances weren't everything? All Justin's fighting happened on the inside where nobody, not even his father and especially not Jessica, could see it. Maybe it was the same way for Jon Hale.

Justin knew that some of the other kids from both of their churches thought it was strange that he and Jon didn't spend more time together since their fathers had become such close friends. He had tried a couple times to arrange some one-on-one time, but Jon always seemed to have something else to do. Always. Justin wasn't offended, exactly. He knew it wasn't anything personal, at least he hoped it wasn't. Jon was busy. Popular. Lots of kids wanted to hang out with him…even though he was annoyingly vocal about his beliefs.

Anyway, he really hadn't minded up until now, because he was nervous about getting too close to his father's new friend's son. What if they didn't get along? What if all Jon wanted to do was discuss the gifts of the Spirit? Justin wasn't scripturally prepared for such a conversation and he knew it. He had little doubt, though, that Jon was prepared. More than prepared.

But he supposed he couldn't avoid him forever. Couldn't, and shouldn't.

"Hey, Jon," he ventured when there was a lull in conversation around the table, "do you want to go shoot some baskets or something with me after school today?"

"Can't," Jon said. "Cross country practice."

"Oh."

"But we'll do it," Jon said. Then he turned to Kyra and whispered, "There's the kid I talked to at the coffeehouse." He pointed to the doorway of the cafeteria where a couple of boys were standing and talking.

"Zeke?" Justin asked. "Zeke went to your coffeehouse?"

"You know him?" Jon seemed surprised.

"I guess I know about him," Justin said. "I've never actually talked to him. His dad used to be a pastor, or something."

Jon's expression was first skeptical and then interested. "Who told you that?"

"One of my teachers when we first moved here," he said. "I told him my dad was a pastor and he shook his head and said, 'Great. Just what I need. Another stressed out, messed up, preacher's kid like Zeke.'"

"Wow," Jon said, more to himself than to anyone else. "That fits."

"Fits?" Justin didn't understand. "Fits what?"

Jon laughed. "Nevermind."

"Trust me," said Kyra. "Nevermind. Unless you want to start talking about the ways God does and doesn't speak in the current church age."

"Well," Justin said, "I guess we will have to talk about that eventually."

Kyra grinned. "I think you should leave that

conversation for your fathers."

"They're not talking about it," Jon said.

"What are you guys talking about?" Will wanted to know.

Jon looked at Justin. Justin looked at Jon. Kyra looked at both of them, and then all three of them looked at Will.

Nevermind.

"Are you coming tonight, Will?" Shayna asked.

Everyone looked at Will again. Would he let his question go to answer Shayna's and save them all a very uncomfortable lunch? Justin hoped so. Talking to Jon one-on-one was one thing. They both already understood why they disagreed. But Will didn't. And he didn't need to. Not this soon.

Will shrugged and redirected his attention to Shayna. "Yeah," he said. "I'll be there."

Relieved, Justin picked up his fork and got to work on his burrito.

* * *

When eight o'clock had come and gone, and then nine o'clock, and Will Cooper still hadn't shown up at the coffeehouse, Shayna began to feel a strange uneasiness. He'd told her he'd be there. Face to face. She told herself that she was overreacting because of what she knew about Will and his father. Maybe they'd gone somewhere together. Maybe Will had gotten a headache.

It was useless. The unnerving feeling…fear, was it?…would not be dismissed.

But the coffeehouse was too busy that night for her to do anything about it. She had been trying for an hour to get a word in to Jon about it, but he'd been talking to someone else.

He stopped talking, though, when Joe/Zeke walked in.

So did Justin Corelli.

Zeke walked slowly into the room, lingered nervously for a moment near the book rack, and then approached Jon. "Got a minute?"

"Sure." Jon stood, nodded to Justin who stood too, and followed Zeke to an empty table.

Curious about what he could be wanting to say, Shayna moved as inconspicuously as she could toward them and sat at a nearby table.

"You," Zeke began, and then cleared his throat to start again. "The last time I was here and you said all that stuff to me about running and all?"

Jon nodded.

"I…you were right."

"Joe," Jon said, "let's—"

"My name isn't Joe. You were right about that, too. My name is Zeke. Zeke Hudson." He glanced at Justin. "I guess Justin here knows that already on account of we've got the same Math class."

"Yeah," Justin said. "I know your name."

"Why'd you tell me otherwise?" Jon asked Zeke.

"I don't know," Zeke said. "I guess I wanted to be anonymous." He glanced at Justin again, and he seemed to Shayna to be glaring, almost.

But she couldn't be sure.

"Anyway," Zeke said, "I might as well be honest

with you since you already figured out that stuff you said about me."

"I didn't figure it out," Jon said. "It was…"

"God," Zeke said. "Yeah. Okay. God. Anyway, my dad was a pastor. He had an affair a couple of years ago. When he went to repent, everyone in the church turned against him. How could he do that to them. A man of God. His poor wife. What a sinner. All that." He shook his head as he looked down at the tabletop. "They were horrible to him. Yeah, what he did was wrong, but it wasn't any more right of them to…to…"

Shayna watched as Zeke pushed his chair back, shook his head again, and stepped away from the table. His face had paled and the muscle above his right eye had begun to twitch. "You know what? I can't do this. I can't."

Before anyone could move to stop him, Zeke ran through the tables, right by Shayna, and out of the coffeehouse into the dark night.

Both Jon and Justin ran after him, but they came back a few minutes later, discouraged. They hadn't been able to find him.

"I kind of overheard you guys," Shayna confessed, going to Jon. "Are you okay?"

"It's not me I'm worried about right now," he answered.

"Maybe he'll come back again," she offered.

"I hope so," he said.

One of the other coffeehouse staff went to the microphone and began a short devotion. Shayna, Jon, and Justin found a table and sat down together, but Shayna suspected that none of them even heard the man.

* * *

After a few moments of indecision about what she was going to do, Raylene Finch glanced around the corner again at her husband. Satisfied that he'd be lost for at least another half hour in the outdoor magazine he was reading, she quietly shut the door to their room and went to the edge of the bed. She stared at the phone for a moment before picking it up.

But she did pick it up.

When her friend Nina, one of the other board members' wives, answered, Raylene chatted for a few minutes about an upcoming church function and then cautiously approached the subject that had really motivated her to call. "Molly Avery came by my house today," she said.

"Oh?"

Nina's tone revealed no discomfort, so Raylene continued. "The poor thing is horribly upset about being told she can't have her wedding at the church."

"Oh?"

"Well, can you blame her?"

A pause. A long one. Then, "I suppose not." Another pause. "You know, Ray, it is a little nonplusing that the man would permit a whole church-full of people who don't believe as we do into our building and not Molly Avery's fiancée."

Nonplusing? Nina must have given this a lot of thought already, Raylene concluded. She wasn't sure nonplusing was even a word. But she was sure now of Nina's take on the situation.

She chose her words carefully. "Oh, Nina, he's not saying Kent can't enter the building."

"You know what I mean."

Raylene's turn to pause. "Yes. I know what you mean."

"What's Bruce going to do about it?"

This was a question that Raylene had not anticipated. One she hadn't even thought to ask herself, or her husband, yet. "I guess he could talk to Pastor Corelli, Nina, but the man is adamant."

"Adamantly ridiculous, if you ask me. I've talked to Sandra already, and Lizette. Everyone agrees with me."

"You know, Nina," Raylene said, "Bruce isn't the only one who can talk to Pastor Corelli. Rick can, too."

"Oh, he's going to. You can be sure of that. And if Molly Avery comes by your house again, you can tell her we'll have this mess settled shortly."

That's what Raylene had been wanting to hear. Poor Molly had been so upset.

* * *

Stomping out the cigarette he'd been too edgy to enjoy, Zeke Hudson looked up at the night sky and shut his eyes.

That had been difficult. Much more difficult than he had imagined.

But he had done it. Taken the first step, anyway.

He felt good about that. He did.

But the good he felt was stiflingly choked by the pain he felt, still, for his father.

"I'm going to get right for you, Dad," he whispered, hating the sting of the tears at his eyes. "I am. I've wasted enough time."

* * *

Jon Hale sat still through the devotion, but his mind was anything but still, and as soon as the teaching was finished he stood to leave. "Want to ride with me, Justin? I'm going to go check on Will."

"Sure." Justin jumped up instantly.

"Great. Maybe we can get started on that conversation you were talking about earlier."

"Great," Justin said.

Yeah, great, Jon thought. The last thing he was in the mood for after his complete failure with Zeke was a doctrinal debate with Pastor Corelli's son. But he supposed it was bound to happen sooner or later, and now was as good a time as any.

Jon led Justin out to his father's 4x4, which Justin appreciatively acknowledged.

"This is the car your dad drove me off the mountain in," he said.

"You remember that?"

Justin nodded. "He saved my life. Him and Corey."

"You must have been really scared," Jon said.

"I was."

Jon climbed in behind the wheel and waited while Justin buckled in beside him.

"The thing that most impressed me about your dad is how calm he was," Justin said. "He just took over and got us out of there."

"He's got a level head. That's for sure."

Justin stared out his window for a few minutes. "You know what amazes me?"

"What?"

"That two men like our dads, both of them totally committed to living for God, could disagree about something as major as what the baptism in the Holy Spirit is."

"It's not that major," Jon said. "I mean, it doesn't affect our salvation one way or the other."

"Yeah," Justin said. "But it's pretty major in how it affects our understanding of finding out God's will."

Jon thought about that. "That's true, I guess."

"I don't want us to fight about it, though," Justin said.

"Good," Jon said, relieved. "I don't want us to, either." He decided that he might as well be honest with Justin. "I guess that's why I've kind of not been in a hurry to spend a lot of time with you. I thought you'd want to fight about it."

Justin laughed. "You did? That only proves that you don't know me very well. You're a lot more outspoken than I'll ever be about anything."

"I didn't know, is all," Jon said. "And I didn't want us messing things up between our dads. Your dad's friendship has been a huge blessing to my father. And he's needed it, especially since the church got burned down."

"I understand," Justin said. "And trust me. I won't complain if we never talk about the gifts of the Spirit."

Jon laughed. "I'm sure we'll want to someday."

"Yeah, like after seminary."

Jon turned onto Will's street. "Is that what you're planning to do? Seminary?"

"I don't know," Justin said. "I want to do something for God. I just don't know what yet, and it's kind of hard to figure out what He wants. It would be so cool if He would just come to me at night like He did to Moses and say 'Go to Pharaoh' or whatever. But He doesn't do that anymore."

"He can," Jon said before he thought better of it. Then he apologized. "We weren't going to talk about that."

"Right," Justin said.

"Here's Will's."

Both boys laughed a little as they got down out of the car and walked up the gravel driveway toward Will's house. Will's truck was parked there, but not Mr. Cooper's. Lights were on inside, Jon could see, and he quickened his pace, not sure why. He'd been telling himself all night that Will hadn't come to the coffeehouse because he'd gone to do something with his father instead. But if he had, the house would be dark now. The fact that it wasn't intimidated him.

He ran up the steps and knocked hard at the screen door. The inside door was open, but Jon couldn't see anyone and the place was completely quiet.

"That's weird," Justin said after they'd waited a couple of minutes and knocked a few more times at the door. "They wouldn't just leave with the place open like this, would they?"

"I wouldn't," Jon said.

"Should we go in? Maybe something's wrong."

For Justin Corelli, who knew nothing about Will Cooper and his father, to say that... slowly, Jon pulled open the screen door and stepped inside. "Will? Mr. Cooper?" He heard Justin come in behind him. "I'll go look upstairs," he said. "You check down here."

Justin nodded even though he was visibly uncomfortable about wandering uninvited through someone's house.

Jon wasn't comfortable, either, but he hurried up the stairs.

9

"Where did the guys go?" Kyra asked Shayna Quinn as she sat beside her. The coffeehouse noise made it necessary for her to pull her chair right up beside Shayna's at the table. "Looking for Zeke again?"

"No," Shayna said. "They went to check on Will."

Kyra nodded. Though she'd been told no details about Will Cooper, she had pieced together that all wasn't well with his family life, and she hoped Jon and Justin would find him home in front of a baseball game.

"So," Shayna said, "you and Justin seem pretty close."

Kyra laughed. "That was random."

Shayna smiled. "I know. It's just that you and I haven't had too many opportunities to get to know one another when everyone and their sister wasn't around." She leaned closer. "Are you guys dating?"

"No," Kyra said. "But he is a good friend. How about you and Jon?"

"The same."

Kyra thought about Justin and about Jon Hale and wondered what they might have talked about on their way to Will Cooper's house. Sports? Church? Their fathers? Music?

Music. Now there was something that Kyra had been doing quite a bit of thinking about during the past week. "Shayna, can I ask you something about your church?"

Shayna seemed to stiffen, just a little, but she smiled easily enough. "Sure."

"I stayed after our service Sunday to help my dad tidy up the fellowship hall, and I kind of over-heard your music service."

Shayna nodded. "I know you guys don't do that the same way we do." She paused to push her napkin forward on the table. "What did you think?"

"I thought it was kind of cool," was all Kyra wanted to say. "I didn't even know that people sang about God in anything but hymns or Christmas music."

Shayna laughed. "Oh, Kyra. You're kidding. There's all kinds of contemporary Christian music. Not just worship stuff, either. Regular music, only it's about Jesus."

"Really?"

"Yeah."

"I wonder why I…why we don't listen to it."

Shayna raised her hands. "You'll have to ask your father about that, Kyra. I'm not even interested in going there. All I know is that it's something about satanic rhythms."

"Satanic rhyth—?"

Shayna held up her hands. "Ask your dad."

Kyra nodded. "I will." Then she shrugged. "There's got to be more to it than that."

"Talk to your dad and let me know what he says. I'd be kind of interested, myself."

"So do you listen to it?" Kyra asked. "The music about Jesus?"

"My parents won't let me listen to anything else."

"It's kind of funny," Kyra said thoughtfully, "how we have all these differences when we all read the same book."

"I doubt that *funny* would be the word God would choose."

* * *

"Will?" Justin stepped around a dining room chair. "Mr. Cooper?" The wood floor squeaked beneath his weight. It was a squeak he never would have heard, he knew, had he not been walking through this house without permission. Everything, even his own breathing, sounded louder than usual in the silent house. "Will?"

He was just about to turn around after poking his head into the kitchen and tell Jon that nobody was around when he saw the broken pitcher and the spilled juice on the floor.

Maybe Will or Mr. Cooper had cut himself on

the splintered glass? Maybe they'd run out in a hurry, anxious to get to the ER?

That would explain why the house had been left open.

"Mr. Cooper?" Justin stepped into the kitchen.

And saw Will, lying, unmoving, on the floor. "Jon," he yelled as he ran to Will and knelt beside him. "Down here."

Will was breathing and didn't seem to be bleeding anywhere, but he wouldn't answer Justin's repeated calls, and that scared him.

"Hurry, Jon!"

"Right here." Jon ran into the kitchen, stopped short at the door for a moment, and then joined Justin beside Will. He reached out to shake him, but Justin held his arm.

"We don't know what happened to him so…"

"Justin," Jon said, "Will's dad beats him."

Justin stared disbelieving at Jon, but then shook it off. "Okay, but his neck might be hurt. We can't move him."

"All right." Jon leaned forward until his face was right at Will's. "Will," he shouted. "Can you hear me?"

Will didn't move.

A noise behind them, the door smacking open against the wall behind it, startled Justin and he jumped to his feet. He stepped back as Mr. Cooper ran into the room, followed by Pastor Hale.

"He won't wake up," Mr. Cooper kept saying, pacing a circle and holding his hands to his head. "How could I have done this to my own son?"

Pastor Hale grabbed Jon's shoulder, nodded toward Mr. Cooper, waited for Jon, who was clearly reluctant to do so, to go to Mr. Cooper, and then knelt beside Will.

"Is he going to be all right?" Justin asked him.

"I don't know yet, Justin," Pastor Hale answered. "Will?"

"Should I call for—?"

Just then, Will tensed and began to cough up vomit. Pastor Hale quickly rolled him onto his side and held his hand firmly on Will's shoulder until he finished. Then he said, "Will, we're here. You're going to be okay." Looking up at Justin, he nodded.

Justin glanced around the room and then ran back toward the living room.

"They don't have a phone," Jon called to him. "There's a cell phone in Dad's…"

Justin didn't listen to the rest. He ran outside, found the cell phone in the drawer underneath the front passenger seat, and called 911. By the time he reentered the house, Will was sitting up, leaning against Pastor Hale, and Jon was sitting on the floor beside Mr. Cooper, insisting to him that God could, and would, forgive him.

Justin decided to go help Pastor Hale. Offering consolation to a man who could beat his son to unconsciousness was not something he cared to do.

"What can I do, Pastor Hale?" he asked.

"Help Jon."

Grimacing, but unwilling to argue with Pastor Hale, he got to his feet, crossed the room, and sat next to Jon beside Mr. Cooper.

* * *

Ed Cooper couldn't breathe. He couldn't hear. He couldn't see anything except Will dropping the pitcher, looking at him with the fearful expectation of certain violence, hurrying to say he'd clean it up, slipping, and smacking his head against the granite counter top.

And then lying there.

Not answering.

"He wasn't doing anything wrong," he said.

"Mr. Cooper," one of the boys was saying, right in his face. Pastor Hale's son. "Mr. Cooper, Will's awake now. The paramedics are on their way. Dad's here. It's going to be okay."

Ed looked at the other boy.

Condemnation. That's what he saw there. So he turned back to Pastor Hale's son. "Will's awake?"

Jon nodded.

"Why'd you hit him?" the other boy wanted to know.

"I didn't."

"Why'd you push him, then?"

"Justin, that's enough," Jon said. "It doesn't matter."

But Ed wanted to answer. "I didn't push him, either. He slipped."

Now Jon was looking at him with condemnation.

So was Pastor Hale.

But then Will said, "He didn't touch me."

"Come on, Will," Jon said. "It's way past the covering up for him stage."

"He didn't touch me," Will repeated.

"So why's he asking me—asking God—how he could do this to his son?" Jon demanded.

"Because I made him afraid," Ed said. Angry emotion burned at his eyes and all the way down his throat, but he had to say it. It was true and he had to say it. He had done this to Will.

"I dropped the juice," Will said. "I looked at him because I knew he'd be upset. The house has to be kept nice because my mother liked it nice. I was going to get something to clean it up. I must have slipped. I remember falling back and then waking up just now."

Ed watched his son.

"He never touched me, Pastor Hale," he said. "I guess I thought he was going to. But he never did."

"So this was an accident," Pastor Hale said.

"No," said Ed. "It was no accident. He thought I was going to hit him because up until you came along I would have. He had every reason to think that. Don't you get it?"

"But you didn't do anything this time, sir," Will said.

Hearing those words from his son, a boy who had found safety in the care of another father but never in his care, twisted Ed's own insides against himself until he thought he would throw up. But he reined in his self loathing enough to get to his feet, cross the room, and sit cautiously beside his son and Pastor Hale.

"Will," he said. But he had to start again because his voice hadn't come. "Will, I...I'm sorry."

It was then, when he heard the words out loud in his own voice, that he knew how inadequate they were. How inadequate they would always be. And as he watched his son lean more heavily against Pastor Hale and shut his eyes, he knew also that it was going to take a lot more than words to even partially piece together his son's shattered trust.

If it could be done at all.

"He didn't touch me, Pastor Hale," Will said. "You've got to make sure the paramedics and everyone understand that."

"I will, Will," Pastor Hale assured him. And then he looked at Ed. "We're going to work you two through this, okay? You two are going to work you two through this."

"I don't see how."

"God sees," Will said.

"God?" Ed said, suddenly cold. "God wouldn't have anything to do with me, Will."

"Hold on, Mr. Cooper."

Ed closed his mouth and looked at the boy beside Jon. Justin.

"God will accept anyone who turns to Him," he said. Then, slowly, he added, "Whatever they've done."

"That's why He had to send Jesus to earth," Jon said. "Because all of us have done wrong."

Ed opened his mouth to object, but allowed himself to be stayed by Pastor Hale's raised hand.

"Ed," the man said, "I know what you're thinking. 'Yeah, but not everyone has done what I've done.'" He looked straight at Ed, and it felt to Ed like he was looking through him. "Am I right? That's what you were thinking?"

"Yeah."

"Any wrong separates us from God," Pastor Hale said. "Any wrong. Big or little. I'm not going to soften anything for you. What you've done in response to your wife's death and your wrong understanding of Will's responsibility in it is reprehensible. It's going to leave scars in Will, and in you, even if you never do anything to him again. It's just going to. That's the way it is. But it's not something that cannot be forgiven. By God." He squeezed his arm tightly around Will's shoulder. "Or by your son."

The paramedics arrived then and everything went a little crazy for Ed Cooper. He rode to the hospital in Pastor Hale's 4x4, waited in the ER waiting room with him, and then rode home in his back seat with Will beside him. He thanked Pastor Hale and the two boys for being there for his son and him and shut his door after them. He helped his son up to his room, where he sat beside him all night and well into the next day.

But even in all the craziness, in all the confused emotion, there was a constant promise in front of him. He'd heard it in Pastor Hale's voice. He'd seen it in Will's life. *God Is.* And he felt it somewhere so deep within himself that he knew it couldn't be anything but true.

God is ready to forgive.

Sometime Saturday afternoon while his son slept inches away from him, Ed Cooper reached out for that promise, and it embraced him.

10

After his father's service Sunday morning, Justin waited in the entryway instead of going downstairs to the Fellowship Hall. He wanted to talk to Jon Hale. He'd done a lot of thinking during the day and a half since leaving Will's house and he figured he had a bit of apologizing to do.

He'd come down way too hard on Mr. Cooper. Smugly. As if he himself had never sinned and had a right to judge the man. Yes, what Ed Cooper had done was inexcusable. Sinful. Wrong. But who was Justin Corelli to look down his nose at another sinner? The only difference between them was that Justin understood that he had a savior.

And maybe that made his sin even worse. Because he knew right from wrong and he knew what it had cost God to make right from wrong with his life and yet he still did wrong sometimes.

He didn't know. He hadn't been able to work

through all of it. He only wished he had behaved more like Jon and Pastor Hale had. Looking for reconciliation. Like God would.

And more than that, he couldn't help thinking of the strange circumstances that God had undoubtedly orchestrated to get him and Jon Hale together to share the gospel with Ed Cooper. With anyone, really, considering their doctrinal differences. All of which had seemed secondary during those moments when they were face to face with a very lost man with the potential to impact him. Mr. Cooper hadn't fallen on his knees in repentance. In fact, he hadn't acknowledged Jon and Justin's words at all. But they had said them. Together.

Who would have thought?

Justin smiled. His father would have thought. And Pastor Hale.

When he saw Jon run up the stairs and hold open the door for his parents, he hurried over to them.

"Do you have a minute?" he whispered to Jon after saying hello to Pastor and Mrs. Hale.

"Just one," Jon said. "I've got to help get the instruments set up."

For the briefest instant, the thought of instruments in church—because he knew that Jon wasn't talking about an organ or a flute—troubled Justin. But he quickly shook the feeling off. It was no mystery that Pastor Hale and his father saw things differently when it came to what was and wasn't worship. And that issue had nothing to do with what Justin wanted to speak with Jon about now.

"I was wrong the other night," he began, "to be

so high and mighty to Mr. Cooper."

"Hey," Jon said, placing his hand on Justin's shoulder, "I felt the same way. Believe me. The guy's the worst kind of...well, you know. But God can forgive him and turn things around for him." He shrugged. "And between him and Will."

"I hope He will," Justin said.

Jon grinned. "If anyone can, it's Him." Then he looked past Justin into the sanctuary. "I've got to go," he said.

"Right." Justin raised his hand. "See you later." He watched for a moment as Jon took a guitar case from someone and hurried toward the platform with it.

Curious about what their worship would actually sound like, but intimidated by the thought that he could hang around and find out, he made his way quickly to the stairs and joined his parents in the Fellowship Hall.

* * *

Alec's right hand tightened around his Bible and sermon notes as soon as he stepped past the open door into the sanctuary. His worship team was up on the platform, plugging in and setting up instruments, microphones, and music stands. And laughing.

"Careful with that thing, Trav," Becca, one of the singers, sarcastically warned the worship leader. "It's sacred."

"It's a chalice," Travis said. "I don't think they actually even use it."

"But it's sacred," Becca repeated. Then she laughed.

"No, it's not," Jon said.

"Yeah," said one of the other musicians. "Only the candles are."

More laughter.

Even from Jon, and that was more than Alec was willing to tolerate. "Is something funny?" he asked more loudly than he would have needed to as he walked toward the pulpit with his Bible.

"No," Travis said, tapping a percussion instrument against his palm.

Becca suddenly needed to review something on one of her sheets of music.

Jon just stood there, unwilling to look directly at him.

The fact that these people, including his own son, knew that they should be uncomfortable about what they had been talking about but had talked about it anyway infuriated Alec almost more than the fact of their talking about it had. "Good," he said, calmly. "Because nothing looked funny to me." He set his Bible on the pulpit and stood there looking at his worship team until each member of it mustered the guts to look back at him. "My guess is that it's a lot bigger of a stretch for Pastor Corelli's people to tolerate our instruments here than it is for us to be respectful of theirs even if they're just cups and candles to us."

"You're right," Jon said. "Sorry."

Becca muttered something similar. Travis just kept his mouth shut. It wasn't exactly the response

Alec had been hoping for, but he knew that he'd earned their obedience even if not their agreement. They wouldn't mock Paul's 'instruments' of worship anymore.

"I guess maybe a sermon out of Romans 14 might be in order sometime," he said, and stepped down from the platform.

He needed to find somewhere quiet to get over being irritated before he preached. He doubted that the worship service, which is where he normally focused his mind on the Lord, would provide anything but frustration today.

"Dad, wait up."

Alec slowed his pace but didn't look back at Jon.

"Dad…"

Now Alec spun around to face his son. "Jon," he whispered, "what were you thinking?" He knew that he'd allowed more of his anger into the question than he normally would have because it was Jon he was asking and not one of the other musicians. Jon knew his commitment to making this arrangement work with Paul's church. Jon knew how he felt about bickering in the church about unimportant little things. And he'd thought that Jon had learned to be better than that, if not from him, from his own work at the coffeehouse.

"I guess I wasn't thinking," Jon said.

Alec accepted the answer, let out a tense breath, and lightly pushed at the side of Jon's head with the heel of his hand. Then he smiled. "I guess you weren't."

"Do you think any of them heard us?"

"That's not even this issue, son."

"I know. But, if they did it could be bad."

"I don't think any of," he raised his hands as quotation marks, "*them* heard you. No."

"Good," Jon said, "because I know how I feel when I hear other Christians making fun of something I believe. It's almost worse than when non-believers do, even if they're saying the same thing."

"There's no almost about it," Alec said. "It is worse because the church is supposed to be one. Not divided against itself over things like candles and banners. Now if someone starts telling you that Jesus was a reincarnation of Adam, then bicker away. But…"

"They are wrong, though, Dad." Jon stared carefully up at him. "We worship God with our hearts, not with…"

"Loud music?" Alec supplied. "Followed by just the right amount of silence?"

Jon grinned and shook his head. "Point taken."

"Good." He smiled. He figured he'd worked most of the irritation out of his heart. "Come greet people with me," he said to his son. "It's just about time to get started."

* * *

Zeke Hudson waited near the stairway until he saw Jon Hale walk up to the platform and grab his guitar before going in to find a seat. He wanted to sit near the back so he could leave as soon as the service was over. And he wanted to sit alone.

Unfortunately, the place was full. Even the front pews.

He smiled. The front pews had always been empty at his father's church. Too close to the spoken Truth for comfort. Apparently the people of Jon Hale's father's church didn't mind being close to the preacher. Or maybe Jon Hale's father never said anything to make people squirm.

He'd see. Soon enough.

He found a pew near enough to the back that had room for him and slid in beside a kid he knew from school. Will Cooper. Will looked awful, Zeke took the time to notice. Tired. A little pale. Tense.

"What's going to happen?" the man on the other side of Will wanted to know.

Will shrugged. "He's going to pray, we're going to sing, and then Pastor Hale will preach."

"Sing?" The man shifted on the pew.

Zeke grabbed a hymnal and busied himself in its pages to hide his amusement at the man's apparent surprise. Of course they'd sing. This was church.

What they'd sing...that was what Zeke was wondering. Hymns? He didn't think so. There was an overhead projector aimed at a blank wall and someone sitting beside it with a pile of transparencies on her lap.

Worship choruses. That's what they'd sung at his father's church. Worship choruses. Only they'd had slide projectors mounted to the ceiling and had flashed the words onto two white screens on either side of the platform. On either side of his father. They'd been getting ready to switch all of that over to computer projected images, though, when his father had confessed his sin and the church had…

Zeke fumbled to slide the hymnal back into its slot on the back of the pew in front of him and then wiped his hands on his pants. Cold sweat.

Pastor Hale went to the pulpit and opened the service in prayer.

Then they were singing.

We love You, Lord. Make our lives pleasing to You. We look to You. Thank you.

Zeke was shaking by the time the worship team left the platform. It had been a mistake to come. He knew that now. But he didn't want to walk out. Pastor Hale was at the pulpit again. He would see him leave. Will Cooper would see him leave.

Zeke recalled one time in his father's church when someone had tried to run out and his father had called to him right from the pulpit. *You can run from this word, son, and you can run from this building and from me and from everyone here. You can even run from yourself. But you can not run from God.*

Zeke shut his eyes and forced himself to breathe in and then out again. Twice. He would not run. Not now. Even when the sermon was over and Pastor Hale had said amen, Zeke didn't run. He simply stood and walked out of the church.

* * *

Usually, Travis Macomb liked to pick something on his guitar after service. Sort of as background noise for all the people leaving and as something to focus on for all the people who had responded to Pastor Hale's message with a request for prayer. There were people praying this afternoon, several of them, but Travis' only thought was getting his guitar put away and getting it and himself out of the building as quickly as possible.

He'd had the whole sermon to think about Alec's comments. He sneered. Alec hadn't *commented,* he'd *rebuked.* And even after chewing on what he'd said for an hour, Travis still couldn't bring himself to swallow it.

Why would his pastor support something as ridiculous as giving honor to candles and cups and snuffers? It was crazy! There was nothing sacred about anything in a church building. It was all just stuff. Material things. And here was his pastor, his friend, his co-minister, correcting him. The worship leader, for crying out loud. No, not correcting him, *embarrassing* him, in front of his worship team. People who looked up to him.

As if Alec Hale knew more about what worship was and wasn't than Travis did!

Crazy. That's what it was.

He'd have to have words with Alec. They were supposed to be team players. If Travis had some kind of beef, any kind of beef, with Alec's new pastor friend, he expected Alec to side with him. Because he was right, for one. And secondly, he'd worked his behind off to get this worship ministry off the ground for Alec. They'd had one guitar and a piano player when he'd first come to Alec's church, and they'd still been singing choruses from the dark ages. Travis had revolutionized and brought life to this church's worship format and it had attracted lots of members for Alec. Tithing members.

How dare Alec challenge him like that in front of his worship team? In front of everyone in the place?

He'd have to have words with Alec. And if Alec wouldn't listen, he'd figure something else out to get his attention.

Their 'instruments' of worship.
Please.

* * *

On the sidewalk outside the church—*her* church—Molly Avery commanded her face to smile at some of the others who'd just left Pastor Hale's service even though a smile was the furthest thing from her heart.

The thought that Pastor Corelli could allow that man to preach in their building—*her* building— when he wouldn't allow her to have her wedding there! She could kick something.

She had never seen such a display of outright craziness. People raising their hands. Singing with their eyes shut. Crying. Shouting Amen whenever they felt like it. One person had even had the audacity to laugh. Right in the middle of a song. True, there had been no snakes, no aerobics, though some people did move a little while they sang, and no prophesies or exorcisms, but it had been weird all the same.

She hadn't paid much attention to what the

people were singing or even to Pastor Hale's message. She'd simply wanted to see for herself what this other church was all about.

And now that she had, she had no intention of keeping quiet about it.

* * *

As soon as he saw his father and Mr. Cooper leave the sanctuary, Jon Hale hurried toward Will and sat beside him. "You doing okay, Will? You don't look good."

"I smacked my head on a granite countertop a couple days ago, remember?" Will grinned. Forced.

"Yeah. I remember." Jon kept looking right at Will even though his friend's strained expression was unnerving him a little. "Your dad came today," he said. "That's really cool."

"Yeah," Will muttered. "I guess."

"What do you mean you guess? It means he's thinking about…"

"It means," Will said coldly, "that he asked me to pray with him yesterday to become a Christian. So now he's coming to church like he thinks he's supposed to."

Stunned by both the news that Mr. Cooper had prayed to receive Christ and by Will's apparent disinterest if not outright hostility about it, Jon decided to lean back in the pew for a moment and think about what he ought to say before opening his mouth. Finally, he said, "You don't seem very happy about that, Will."

"I...I just don't..." Will rubbed at his temples as he shook his head. Without looking at Jon, he said, "I just don't think I can do this, Jon. Now he's a Christian and I'm a Christian and I'm supposed to just forgive him and go to church with him and love him like nothing ever happened?" Again, he shook his head. "It's too hard. It's too weird."

"Do you think he really meant it?" Jon asked. "When he prayed?"

"Yeah," Will answered right away. "He meant it."

"So it's not that you don't trust his motives."

Will shook his head. "He meant it."

"It's your part you're having a hard time with."

Slowly, as if he felt ashamed, Will nodded.

Jon placed his hand on Will's arm and waited for him to look at him. "Nobody expects it not to take time. Your father's decision doesn't change that."

"It doesn't?"

"No."

"Well," Will said, clearly struggling to grab some solace out of Jon's words, "maybe things'll look different to me when this headache lets up some." He leaned forward and rubbed at his eyes with the heels of his hands. "I mean, it really is cool that my father...that he..."

Jon stood. Will looked ready to throw up. "Come on. I'll run you home."

"My father..."

"I'll tell him."

"He won't appreciate the interruption."

Frustrated, Jon sat beside Will again. "Listen to me," he said. "All that stuff you said about how you should be treating your father now that he's a Christian? Well it applies to him too now, and I'm guessing he knows it. He's not going to be angry if I take you home. God is able, Will. You've got to believe that."

But as Jon walked his friend out to his truck and then went back inside to look for their fathers, he had to wonder. Not whether God was able. Of course He was. But Will and his father would have to give Him room.

11

Paul Corelli startled to see snow falling outside his office window when he looked up from his counseling journal at the end of what had been a very long Monday at the beginning of October.

He'd spent all day in counseling sessions, and it seemed to him that nearly everyone had wanted to talk about him and his problems rather than their own.

"Lots of people are talking, Pastor."

"I heard Molly and Kent haven't found another place to have their wedding yet."

"Somebody told me that Pastor Hale believes in Christians being demon possessed. Do you think he does?"

"My kids said that Jessica's been having a hard time getting along with her teachers."

"It would be a shame to see you get voted out."

Paul had assured each of them that people would always talk, that there was always the Justice of the

Peace if Molly and Kent ran out of options, that Alec did not believe that Christians could be demon possessed—and it wouldn't be any of our business if he did, that he and Rose were well aware of Jessica's current struggles and were dealing with them, and that he had no intention of being voted out, thank you very much for your concern.

After finishing up the last of his notes, he shut his journal and slid it into his desk drawer. Then he stood to stretch his back.

What a day.

As far as he was concerned, things were going extremely well between his church and Alec's. No major blow-outs or misunderstandings. No zealots lurking in the hallways between their two services to slam one another with the most recent Bible verses they'd dug up for or against the present day gifts of the Spirit or music or emotionalism or whatever. He and Alec couldn't be getting along better even if they believed the same way about everything.

It was just that there were a few malcontents like Molly Avery who had other issues with Paul himself trying to stir up whatever they could of the potential conflict in the situation.

It irritated him, but he had expected it. It concerned him, of course, but not too much because there were other things that concerned him more.

Jessica, for instance.

The person who'd mentioned her today had been exactly on target. Jessica was having trouble getting along with her teachers...and the other students, Justin, and just about everyone else. Including Paul and Rose. He knew that she missed her friends in New York—she missed New York itself. He knew that she hated Montana—there was never anything cool to do. He knew that she resented him for dragging her across the country when she'd asked him, begged him, really, to pass up this church when the Bishop had offered it to him. He knew that she was losing interest in the things of God.

And he knew that he was basically helpless to turn things around for her. She was fifteen years old. No longer a child who would or wouldn't do things because Mommy or Daddy said so. She had to make her own decisions. He and Rose could keep her from going to parties and participating in friendships and lifestyle choices that would constitute outright rebellion against God, but they could not control, and didn't want to, what went on in her mind and heart. She had to do that.

Paul had learned to find peace when it came to raising his children in one place and one place only: on his knees. God was his kids' Father, even more than he was. As much as Paul loved Justin and Jessica, he knew that God loved them more. He had to put them in God's hands. Especially now that they were older. He had to trust Him to be the 'author and finisher' of his children's faith, just as he was trusting Him for himself.

Jessica was a tough case, though. Resentful. Envious of the perceived freedom her 'non-pastor's-kid' friends had. Stuck in self-imposed loneliness. Fighting against God's work in her life.

Paul's thoughts caught in his stomach like a fork

caught in the gears at the bottom of the dishwasher, twisting it.

People weren't talking back and forth about Jessica because they were concerned about her. They were talking about her because they were looking for things to hurl at him. The whole "church leaders must have their children under control with all dignity" thing.

If Jessica blew it, they could vote him out.

That's why they were talking about Jessica.

Because they were upset about Alec's church using their building. And about Molly Avery's wedding.

He thought about the churches in town that had been vandalized recently. Two of them. Broken glass. Anti-Christian literature. Paint. He wondered who these enemies of their faith were. And he wondered if they realized how competent Christians could be at trashing their own work without any help from them.

* * *

Pastor Al Snyder hurried inside the building as soon as the snow began to fall. He'd finished scrubbing all the paint off the walls and sweeping up the broken glass from the sidewalk outside the front door. One of the members of his church who owned a construction business had already come and replaced the door itself and had bagged all the literature that had been tossed inside on the entryway floor. The building looked in order again, but Pastor

Snyder still felt ill at ease.

Who would do something like this to a church? To so many churches? Why? Police still had no clues, and nobody was claiming responsibility. Pastor Snyder had actually considered hiring a security guard to watch his church each Saturday night or installing some kind of alarm system, but had decided against doing either.

Now he was second guessing that decision.

Even so, he knew he had a lot to be thankful for in that his church was still standing. At least it hadn't been burned to the ground like that church on the other side of town had.

He had heard from one of his colleagues that Paul Corelli had opened up his building to the pastor of that church and his people until they could rebuild. A 'Spirit-filled' church. Al had to wonder how—not to mention why—Paul was making it work considering that the two congregations believed so differently about, well, about everything. He couldn't imagine sharing his building with a 'Pentecostal' congregation. There were so many names for the movement but they all meant the same thing to Al Snyder: heretics, wackos, fanatics.

Still, a certain part of him admired Paul Corelli for putting in the effort. Especially considering what had just happened to his own building. Wouldn't he hope that someone would help him if his church had been burned down instead of just vandalized?

Yes. He would.

He'd have to give Paul Corelli a call sometime to offer some support. Some comforting. The situation had to be driving the man insane.

* * *

Alec stepped from the front passenger seat and met Paul on the sidewalk for the quick walk up the stairs and inside. The big old church felt forbidding, but he attributed it to the grayness of the day and tried to dismiss his apprehension. It had snowed all afternoon and through the night but had let up just before he'd left the house to meet Paul for breakfast.

Now his stomach was protesting the fact that he'd eaten.

Or was it the fact that he'd agreed to come to this meeting?

Both, he suspected.

Well, he didn't intend to give it anything else to knot up about. He'd sit beside Paul and keep his mouth shut.

"Pastor Corelli," a white-haired man whose voice Alec recognized from one of the local Sunday morning radio programs he'd had a chance to hear now that he didn't have to be to church until noon said as he approached Paul. "Nice to see you." He looked at Alec. "This must be Pastor Hale?"

Alec smiled and held out his hand. "That's right."

"Come and have a seat. Everyone else is here already."

Alec followed Paul into the ornate sanctuary, not failing to notice the curious glances of the ten or so men who had apparently gotten off to an early start this morning. The meeting wasn't scheduled to begin for another ten minutes.

"Shall we pray?" the white-haired man—Alec struggled for his name and came up empty—said in opening, and everyone present bowed his head. A long monotone prayer thanking God for the opportunity to meet and asking Him to have His will in each of their lives, and then the white-haired man said, "Paul, why don't you introduce your guest?"

Paul stood and indicated to Alec that he should do the same. "This is Pastor Alec Hale. He pastors the…"

"The church you're graciously sharing your building with," one of the men said. "We know."

"Uh, okay," said Paul. He grinned. "So why am I standing up?" He sat down.

This time Alec didn't need any cues from Paul. He sat quickly.

"So how's it going?" someone asked, looking at neither Paul nor Alec but obviously intending the question for either or both of them. "We're all dying to know."

Alec smiled. He couldn't help it. But he didn't answer the question. This was Paul's meeting. His friends and colleagues. He could do the talking.

"It's going very well," Paul said. "Oh, you know, there are the logistical things about getting two hundred people out while two hundred people are trying to come in, but," he shrugged, "I guess any two churches would have that problem."

"But you're not any two churches," the white-haired man said. "At least give yourselves the credit you deserve for what you've undertaken."

"We are any two churches," Paul protested.

"Any two churches will have differences," Alec decided it would be safe to add.

"Besides," Paul said, "we haven't undertaken anything extraordinary. Churches all over the place are working together to reach their communities. It's not that big a deal."

"Ah, yes, Pastor Corelli," the white-haired man said. "But they can always go back to their own places when their joint events are finished."

"It's Paul's church," Alec said.

"Actually," Paul said, looking at Alec, "it's the Lord's church. At least that's my hope."

"Semantics," the white-haired man said. "Do you mean to imply that there haven't been any challenges whatsoever?"

"No," Paul said. "But nothing major."

Alec looked from man to man until he'd made eye contact with each of them. He supposed that they thought they could pinpoint the kinds of conflicts his church and Paul's would encounter, and it saddened him to acknowledge that they probably wouldn't be too far off. He knew that Paul was beginning to get grief from his board, and he had heard a bit of it himself from some of his people. His worship leader, for one, was indignant that Alec hadn't more forcefully taken up the issue of the sacredness—or lack thereof—of Paul's altar items. His youth pastor had found some suspiciously conspicuous anti-tongues literature in the youth room and had complained to Alec that he should complain to Paul who could complain to *his* youth pastor. Alec hadn't said a word to Paul about that or anything else, and he suspected that there were many things Paul hadn't mentioned to him, either.

Most of the people were willing and able to tolerate their differences. But there were always those few in every congregation who seemed to consider it their duty to God and Man to make life as difficult as possible for their pastor, eager to give him every opportunity to prove and re-prove his character.

For the good of the body, of course.

Multiply that by two and that pretty much summed up the situation.

But it was working. Wasn't that the bottom line?

Yes. That was the bottom line. Which is exactly what Paul reiterated to his colleagues until the white-haired man mercifully changed the subject to their annual interdenominational Thanksgiving food drive for the poor and needy.

* * *

Pastor Mel Pearson lowered his newspaper to the coffee table and pressed at his eyes with his knuckles. Another church had been vandalized. This was becoming quite the epidemic, it seemed. And quite the mystery.

Quite the nuisance.

There were only so many churches in town. If these vandals were not caught soon, it was only a matter of time before Mel's church was hit. He laughed. They could 'hit' his church next. That very night, except they seemed to have chosen to 'work' only on Saturdays.

"Did you hear about Pastor Snyder's church?" he asked his wife when she came into the room with the quilt she was working on for one of the new mothers in the church and sat beside him on the couch.

"Yes," she said. "It's so horrible. And so strange. First they vandalized a couple of churches, then they burned Alec's to the ground, and now they're vandalizing again."

"What happened at Alec's church might have been unrelated," he pointed out, although he didn't think so.

"I suppose," his wife said. "Have you seen Alec lately?"

"Pastors' prayer last month," he said.

"What are they doing for a building?"

Mel smiled. How had he forgotten to share *that* bit of information with his wife? "Pastor Corelli—that guy who was inviting all the pastors, Spirit-filled or otherwise, to meet together for prayer—is sharing his building with Alec's church until they can rebuild."

"He's Baptist, or something, isn't he?"

"I'm not sure what denomination he is, but, yeah, basically."

"Hm." She turned over a corner of the quilt to check her stitching.

He grinned at the smile forming at the corners of her mouth. "What?"

"I just can't imagine it. 'You want to bring

drums into our sanctuary, Pastor Hale? I better not walk in and find people lying on the floor, Pastor Hale. Just don't trip and break anything when you prance around with your Bible, Pastor Hale.'" She shook her head. "What a stretch it must be. For both of them, but Alec especially since it's the other guy's building."

"Yeah," said Mel. "It must be."

Personally, Mel didn't think he'd have the backbone for it. He had enough conflict just among his own people, who all supposedly agreed. More so now than in the past since one particular woman and those who agreed with her had split from his church to start their own work. *A place where the Spirit would be free to demonstrate His power.* Mel forced himself to admit that he'd known it was bound to happen sooner or later, and that things really had been a lot better without the constant entryway politics of the discontent few. But still, the split had stolen a huge chunk of his confidence. In himself and in God's calling on his life. And it had rendered him cynical.

But not too cynical to admire Pastors Hale and Corelli. They'd stepped into an inherently difficult situation and were apparently making it work. That said a lot about them. Both of them.

He'd have to give Alec a call. He could probably use some encouragement, some empathy.

* * *

Pastor Terry Stoltz lay awake that night beside

his wife, thinking about the meeting he had attended that morning. About Pastor Corelli's suggestion that they think about a community wide all-churches-welcome-and-participating Christmas Eve service. An idea that he and his friend, Pastor Hale, had been tossing around.

Terry had watched all the men present while Paul outlined how they intended to organize it. Too many of their faces showed skepticism and it hadn't taken long for them to begin putting words to it.

"Who's going to decide which churches will participate?"

"We'll leave it open to anyone who wants to come," Paul had answered.

"You obviously haven't thought this through very far, Pastor Corelli. Do we want cults—" He'd paused to look disrespectfully at Alec Hale. "And everyone else there just because they say they're Christians?"

Alec Hale had stiffened then. And no wonder. But he had held his tongue, which had done more than anything Paul Corelli could have said about him to secure Terry's respect.

Paul had remained resolute in spite of the reactions of the men around him. He'd encountered this before, Terry recalled, and was apparently getting used to it. He hadn't looked bothered at all. He'd simply stated that he fully intended to help Alec organize the service. "We can either make a statement for Christian unity or keep to our divisions," he'd said. "But don't think that the world doesn't notice."

Terry rolled onto his side.

His church would participate in Paul and Alec's service, no matter what his board thought or said. They could grin and bear something a little different for two hours, he figured, or else they could stay home.

12

Justin sat beside his mother and waited for his father to ask the blessing. He couldn't believe it was already Thanksgiving. And he was just as baffled by the odd collection of people around his dining room table. Pastor Hale and his family. Zeke Hudson. Will Cooper and his father. And most perplexing of all, Molly Avery and her fiancée Kent.

He smiled as he looked down at his plate. He knew that his parents didn't like to pass holidays away in sleepy boredom in front of a football game, but this was ridiculous.

Molly Avery?

Hadn't that woman and her wedding been the single greatest thorn in his father's side lately, with the possible exception of their building arrangement with Pastor Hale? Yet his parents had invited her. And she had accepted and had brought along her fiancée!

As his father prayed and as Justin muttered his amen afterwards, he hoped that the meal would be uneventful. Enjoyable seemed to be too much to ask for.

One way or the other, it wouldn't be boring.

"How are the plans for the Christmas service coming along?" Mr. Cooper scooped a healthy portion of mashed potatoes onto his plate. "Were you able to secure use of the arena?"

Pastor Hale nodded—his mouth was full.

Even though Justin thought a facility that could seat five thousand was overly ambitious of his father and Pastor Hale, the idea of having a huge church service there did intrigue him. Everything would have to be big, and loud, and relevant.

Not your typical Sunday morning pray, sing, sit through the sermon, sing again, pray again church service.

"What Christmas service?" Zeke wanted to know.

Jon stopped his knife halfway between the butter dish and his roll. "I didn't tell you about it?"

"Nope."

Jon Hale had been spending a lot of time with Zeke lately. Justin had tried a couple times, too, to talk with Zeke, but it had never gone anywhere. Apparently, Zeke didn't trust anyone but Jon. And, except for Jon, everyone seemed to be feeling the same way about Zeke. It wasn't something that Justin could put a finger on…Zeke did or said such and such and it didn't add up. Nothing like that. It was just a feeling, probably because Zeke was so difficult to read. He'd open up, and then run. Over and over again. He'd come to Christian events and then squirm all the way through them. Jon had told Justin about his supposed 'word of knowledge' about Zeke—that he was running from God. He supposed that that would be a troubling thing to attempt. Impossible to sustain. Something a person would deliberately try to mask. An inside tug of war that was bound to manifest itself in conflicting behavior.

But if Zeke was running from God, why was he hanging around Christians? And if he was struggling to inch his way back toward Him, why hadn't he asked any of those Christians to pray with or for him?

Justin stuffed a bite of stuffing into his mouth. It was beyond him. And none of his business. If God was drawing Zeke back to Himself, which He would undoubtedly try to do, He would take care of putting someone in his face who could discern and disassemble the lies he'd bought into and told.

"My father never would have participated in something like that," Zeke said when Jon had finished describing the premise and plan for the Christmas Eve service.

"Why not?" Jon asked.

Justin suspected that the direction of this conversation was not doing anything to promote the holiday spirit for his father or Pastor Hale. But he looked at Zeke, curious.

"Because." Zeke shrugged. "He would have looked at it like compromise. Watering things down to the lowest common denominator rather than standing for the standard."

"But," Pastor Hale offered, "considering that the 'lowest common denominator' in this case is the message of salvation by grace, stripped of all the extra stuff, we really are uniting under the most important standard."

Zeke thought about that. "I didn't say I'd agree with my dad. That's just what he would have done."

"What do you mean by salvation by grace?" Kent wanted to know.

Molly glanced at him and then looked away rolling her eyes. "I've only explained it to you seven hundred times, Kent."

Justin watched Kent, who didn't flinch from looking at Pastor Hale.

* * *

Kent Sherman listened intently to the man talking to him, Pastor Hale. He wasn't half as drawn in by what he was saying as he was by the belief that was obviously behind it. Kent had, as Molly had told everyone, heard the dissection of what these people called 'salvation by grace.' He understood that they believed that, as sinners, people who did wrong even if only once in a while, we had separated ourselves from God. God, in His mercy, had sent his Son, the man Jesus Christ, to die a horrible death on a cross to make atonement for those sins for anyone who would accept and believe in Him.

Kent could take the scenario only so far. He was a sinner. Well, *sinner* was a religious word. But he did things wrong and he knew it. He did believe that if there was a God, He'd expect a certain standard of doing right. If, anyway, He was any kind of a God worth serving. It was the 'Jesus died on the cross' thing that troubled Kent.

Shouldn't someone have to do something to earn his own acceptance from God?

Something a little more strenuous than saying *Yeah, I believe*?

Molly, for example. Here she was, eating Thanksgiving dinner with her pastor, thinking that she was just as good a Christian as anyone else in the world, when all the while she had been 'sinning' in her relationship with him. Sleeping with him when they weren't married. He knew that it bothered her, the contradiction, but not enough to actually change her behavior. Did she just assume that she was forgiven because she'd said 'I believe' at one point in her life? And he had to wonder how much she really did believe if she wasn't willing to live the things her belief supposedly required.

True, a lot of things in the Bible, which was supposed to be the sacred rule book, weren't perfectly clear. But there was no doubt about its position regarding sleeping with someone when you weren't married. Even Kent, who had never been to church in his life, knew that.

He had simply concluded early on in his relation-ship with Molly that she didn't really believe what she thought she believed as much as she thought she believed it. And he suffered no guilt about helping her to compromise something she only thought she believed because they weren't his beliefs, either. It was just religion. In real life, unmarried people slept together. It's just the way it was. Right? Wrong? Who could say? It was working for him.

But this guy in front of him, Pastor Alec Hale. This was a piece of work. A guy who, from everything Kent had heard and read in the paper, did believe what he said he believed enough to actually live it. That counted for something.

And then it hit Kent. All at once while Pastor Hale was saying something about grace literally meaning 'unmerited favor'.

Living your "Yes, Lord, I believe" would be the thing a person could do to be acceptable to God. A person would have to be given the grace, the unmerited favor, first, because he could never undo the wrong he had already done and would probably still do afterwards. But he could endeavor to live his "I believe" and God would see that, and maybe He'd even help him.

He'd have to give it some thought, he decided as he picked up his roll and began to eat again. Then he looked over at Molly.

Unmerited favor. That's what she'd been living on. Holding on to. He couldn't help wondering if she ever wondered how long God would continue to extend it to her when she was deliberately neglecting her end of the covenant.

Suddenly, her rush to be married made a lot more sense to Kent.

No longer hungry, he returned his roll to his plate.

* * *

As Pastor Hale, Pastor Corelli, and Kent shifted their conversation clumsily from salvation by grace to the current NFL season, Will Cooper looked over at his father. This was the best Thanksgiving he'd ever had. He supposed that his first three, before his mother had died, had been wonderful too, but he didn't remember those. He only remembered the lack of them in their home. Until now.

Things weren't perfect between him and his father yet. His father still became angry and cold at times, but he hadn't hit Will or even come close in months. Will, for his part, sometimes thought he'd actually forgiven his father, but more often still had to battle the conflicting feelings he held about pursuing a "normal" relationship with him. Sometimes, he just wanted to go live somewhere else and make a life for himself without any of this struggle.

But he knew that that wasn't what God would want.

God, it seemed to Will, had worked miraculously in both his and his father's lives just to give their new relationship a start, and even though building on what God had begun by saving both of them was difficult, Will had no intention of wasting any of His effort.

Or the efforts of the two pastors sitting at the table with him. And their sons.

While Will still admired Jon and Justin for their commitment to their lives with God, he no longer envied them their relationships with their fathers.

That was probably the one thing he was most thankful for. Not because he didn't envy them. But because he didn't have as much of a reason to anymore.

He and his father were moving in the right direction. Slowly. Painfully. But they were moving.

* * *

His heel tapped relentlessly against the leg of his chair. His hands had grown so sweaty that he could barely hold onto his fork while he ate. Inside his stomach it felt as if every bite he'd forced past his forced smile into his mouth had turned into a living, starving, scraping mass of claws.

He wanted to run.

But he didn't.

"Are you ready for some pie, Zeke?" Mrs. Corelli asked him.

"No. Thank you. I can't eat another bite." He lifted his plate to his shoulder and she took it from him.

"Anyone else?"

A unanimous groan of *maybe later* went around the table.

Zeke laughed, mostly to relieve the muscles in his face. Forcing it to remain expressionless had taken every ounce of his will. As Pastor Corelli and Jessica stood to help Mrs. Corelli clear the table, Zeke stood too. But he didn't help with the dishes. Instead, he went to the sink and stared through the window at the approaching night. It would be here soon. And as soon as Zeke could think of a way to excuse himself from this house and these people without appearing rude, he would do it.

He needed fresh air.

And he needed to regain control.

13

Pastor Byron Smith watched the sheriff's car pulling away from his church until he could no longer see it through the falling snow. Though it was cold outside, though he was cold, he remained on the cement steps for several minutes before shoving his hands angrily into his pockets and turning to go inside.

Who would do this? On the day after Thanksgiving. And why his church? Why now?

He knew about the vandalism in the community, of course, but he'd pled the blood of Jesus over his building and had claimed that it would be spared from this fiery attack of the enemy.

Well, it hadn't been a fiery attack, exactly. Not the way it had been for Pastor Alec Hale's church. But it was an attack of the enemy, nonetheless.

"Well," he muttered into the thick collar of his coat as he pulled open what was left of the church's front door and stepped inside to find the literature that had been thrown on the floor, "I must be doing something right if Satan is attacking me."

"That's an interesting perspective," a voice said behind him. One he didn't recognize. "I guess a lot of us are doing things right, then." A quick laugh. "Me more than anyone."

Now Pastor Smith recognized the voice and couldn't help allowing a grin. But it completely disappeared by the time he turned fully around to face Pastor Hale and saw Pastor Corelli standing behind him. He'd been hearing a lot about these two men lately from some of his colleagues at the Pentecostal Pastors' Prayer meetings he attended biweekly. Some of what he'd been hearing was positive. *They must be two strong men to pull off sharing a church building like that.* But mostly, his fellow pastors considered Pastor Hale's willingness to subject himself to the whims of Pastor Corelli's non-Spirit-filled board and congregation a weakness. Surely it would be better to meet in homes or in a school gymnasium than to adhere to all the strenuous and dead guidelines that were undoubtedly written into their agreement.

Of course, Pastor Corelli had offered his building. A gesture which hadn't even occurred to Pastor Smith or any of Alec Hale's other like-minded colleagues.

It was then that Pastor Smith recalled his telephone conversation with Pastor Corelli.

"I will not pray where the Spirit is not free to flow," he had declared. He'd been in prayer meetings

before with non-charismatics. Never had he endured anything so boring and ineffectual. A bunch of sleepy looking men calling on a God who, according to their beliefs, no longer had any power or inclination to intervene on their behalf.

At one such meeting, his last, Pastor Smith had taken up a request for a man with cancer, so, naturally, he'd prayed, in the name of Jesus and by His blood and stripes, for a healing. He didn't shout or wail or draw out the 's' at the end of the Savior's name so as not to offend anyone, but he'd offended them nonetheless. Why else would several of them have felt the need to clarify his prayer? How could it be any more clear? *Lord, we claim this man's healing in Your name.* Apparently, he'd neglected to specify adequately enough how, exactly, God would be permitted to accomplish this. Giving the doctors wisdom, for one. Allowing the treatment to be successful, for another. And giving the man strength and emotional well-being during his illness.

Rubbish. That's what those kinds of prayers were. Any and all of those things could happen without God even lifting a finger. Why even bother asking? If you're going to call on Him, why not ask for a flat-out, no-holds-barred, none-could-do-it-but-God, *healing*? Surely He could still perform them!

But that was all secondary to the thing currently at hand: Pastor Corelli's presence at his building.

Pastor Hale held up a broom. "We came to help you clean up," he said. "Heard about your church on the radio."

"Oh, that won't be necessary," Pastor Smith said,

still looking at Pastor Corelli. Was the man simply trying to 'heap coals on his head' for the way he'd treated him on the phone? If so, it would be a wasted effort. Pastor Smith's uncle had been at Azusa Street itself, and his family had seen the power of God then and until now and he had no intention of relenting or apologizing for it. "I'm sure some of my brethren will be along soon."

"We are your 'brethren,'" Pastor Hale said. "Paul, you want to go grab that scrubbing brush you—?"

Suddenly, Pastor Smith felt smallness in his stomach like a rancid chunk of cheese. "I didn't mean that how it sounded," he said. "Thank you for coming. It being a holiday when your families are home, and all."

"No problem." Pastor Corelli smiled and then ran down the steps toward the 4x4 they'd driven over in.

"We might as well clean up outside, first," Pastor Hale said. He zipped his jacket up past his chin. "Then we can warm up by working inside."

"I don't know how warm it will be."

Pastor Hale glanced at the busted-out windows that made up most of the front door and nodded.

The three men worked in silence, scrubbing the obscenities from the outside wall of the church and from the sign at the curb. None of Pastor Smith's 'brethren' showed up, he couldn't help noticing. He wondered if Pastors Corelli and Hale noticed, too.

"How about we take a break and go somewhere warm for a cup of coffee before starting inside?" Pastor Corelli suggested when they'd finished.

Pastor Hale rubbed his hands together in front of his mouth as he breathed out onto them. Then he nodded. "No argument here."

No longer able to feel *his* hands, Pastor Smith reluctantly offered his agreement and the three men walked quickly together toward a café at the end of the block.

* * *

Molly Avery slammed the cupboard door shut and took a moment to steady her breathing before turning to face Kent again. She could not believe what she had just heard him say. True, he'd been acting strangely since they'd gotten back to her apartment last night after their Thanksgiving meal at Pastor Corelli's home, but she could never have imagined or anticipated such a disturbing response to her repeated demands for him to quit his brooding and get to the heart of the matter. "What did you say?" she asked to make certain she hadn't misheard.

He was sitting at the kitchen table, tapping the handle of his coffee mug and glaring at her. "You heard me."

Yes. She had. *Why don't we just live together?*

"That's what I thought." She lowered herself slowly onto the chair beside his and forced herself to look directly at him. "Do you want to tell me where this is coming from? I thought you wanted to get married. I mean, you proposed."

"Yeah," he said, "I proposed."

"But now you've decided you don't love me?"

His expression flashed anger and then dulled to cynical amusement. "It's not about me, Molly. It's about you. Do you want to marry me because you love me or because it's a convenient way to quit feeling guilty about what we're doing?"

"I wouldn't be doing what I've been doing if I didn't love you," she replied through a jaw that wouldn't move.

"Really," he said.

"Yes. Really."

"Let's just say, for the sake of there's nothing else to do right now, that you and those two pastors yesterday and every other Christian out there's who's so willing to condemn us are right about your religion."

"We are right," she said. "Kent, if this is about something someone said yesterday, then…"

"Nobody said anything yesterday," he shouted. "It's just that I finally figured it out, your big rush to get married." He shook his head and laughed coldly. Bitterly. "You want me to be a Christian. You want me to marry you. You know what, though?"

Molly whispered, "What?" even though her entire body had stiffened against whatever it was he was about to say.

"I'm not going to marry you just so you can feel all right in your little Christian world. And if I did become a Christian, I wouldn't marry you anyway because if I became a Christian, it would be because I knew it was true and it would mean everything to me." He pushed his coffee mug toward her, slid his chair back, and got to his feet. "And it obviously doesn't mean everything to you."

Molly moved so quickly to stand as Kent left the room that she banged her thighs on the table, spilling his coffee. "How dare you," she yelled after him. She fell back onto her chair as tears burned at her eyes. "How dare you!"

The trouble was, she knew exactly how.

*   *   *

"So how do you explain all the miracles that happen today?"

"How do *you* explain all the miracles that *don't* happen today, seeing how everyone who was prayed for in the New Testament was healed?"

"That was never given as a promise. It never says, 'And everyone you pray for will be healed.'"

"But it's precedent. That's what's there."

"It's also precedent that everyone in the New Testament who was baptized was baptized in a natural body of water. What does that say about baptismal tanks?"

"Gentlemen." Alec held up his hands. "Please." He looked first at Paul and then at Pastor Smith. He couldn't believe how quickly and irretrievably Pastor Smith had plowed the conversation from the cappuccinos they'd ordered into the doctrine of the gifts of the Spirit. "It might be more productive if you answered some of one another's questions." He kept looking steadily at Paul. "But it's been my experience that these debates are rarely productive, no matter how they're undertaken."

"There's nothing wrong with showing a brother the way more perfectly," said Pastor Smith.

"The gifts of the Spirit were to establish the early church," Paul, who had been challenged and clearly felt up to the task of showing Brother Smith the way more perfectly, said. "Even as early as the writing of the New Testament, they had ceased."

"How do you figure?" Pastor Smith had to know.

Alec leaned back in his chair and raised his cup of coffee to his lips. The steam rising from it, and the rich smell, warmed and relaxed him. Physically. Emotionally, though, he remained on edge. He and Paul had worked diligently, it seemed to him, to avoid this issue, and now they were right in the middle of it with Pastor Byron Smith. Not a pretty picture. But Alec determined to keep silent. He didn't want to weigh the conversation against his friend, but more than that, he suspected he might actually hear Paul's reasoning if he kept himself in the observer mode instead of feeling the need to scrounge his memory for a response to every point.

"Why does Paul instruct Timothy to take wine for his stomach?" Paul was asking. "Why not just pray for him? Why was Epaphroditus left to become sick to the point of death? Why didn't Paul just pray for him?"

"I suppose he probably did."

"Exactly," Paul said. "And he wasn't healed. Because the gifts had ceased."

"Have you thought to take into account the sovereign will of God?" Pastor Smith leaned into the table. "You're assuming that Epaphroditus' failure to be healed proves that the gifts had ceased, but couldn't it just as legitimately prove that everyone who was prayed for in the New Testament *wasn't* healed, putting your precedent theory into question?" He paused. "I can tell you in one scripture, black and white, why I believe what I believe. Can you do the same?"

"Scriptures can be taken out of context," Paul reminded the older pastor. "You have to consider the whole, not just the parts that seem to back up what you want to believe."

"You can't give me a scripture," Pastor Smith concluded, "not one, because there isn't one that says the gifts were only for the first years of the church—"

"First Corinthians 13:8 says, *But as for prophesies, they will come to an end; as for languages, they will cease...*"

"Ah, but Acts 2:39 says, *For the promise is for you and for your children, and for all who are far off, as many as the Lord our God will call.* That's me. And you."

Exactly, Alec thought, but he said nothing.

"The word 'promise' in that scripture is referring to the promise of remission of sins."

"It's referring to the promise of the Holy Spirit as in earlier verses in the 2nd chapter of Acts."

"Even if I gave you that," Paul said, "which I haven't, the 'promise' or 'gift' of the Holy Spirit doesn't necessarily equal the *gifts* of the Holy Spirit." He took in a deep breath and then a sip of his coffee. "I believe this: there are genuine miracles that happen today because God is still God and can do what He wants. But the gift of healing, as it was dispensed in the New Testament, is no longer present. Nobody has the gift to pray for people with the absolute certainty that they'll be healed, but people think they do, and that's where you get into all your abuses of so-called spiritual power."

"You're going back to your precedent thing again. The Bible never *says* that the gift of healing is a guarantee that everyone you pray for will be healed. And it never *says* that one person will have the gift of healing for his entire ministry. In fact, it *says* that God distributes the gifts to each one as He wills. Isn't it possible that the gift of healing could be present one day but not the next?"

"That's not the way it happened in the New Testament."

"Okay." Pastor Smith's turn to sip some coffee. "Okay. What it sounds like you're saying to me is that because there are abuses, the gifts are obviously gone. If the genuine gift was present, there wouldn't be room for abuses."

"Right, because there weren't abuses in the New Testament, when the genuine gift *was* present."

"Then why did Paul have to write to the Corinthians about the way the gifts should be in operation in the church?"

"When the apostles prayed for people, they were healed. There was no working up the faith or blaming sin in their lives if it didn't happen or people falling out in rows at the lifting of someone's hand. The apostles prayed and people were healed. It was that simple. What's going on in a lot of places today is pure fraud."

"I give you the fact that people mess up," Pastor Smith said.

"There was no *messing up* in the New Testament."

"But," repeated Pastor Smith, "should we do away with baptism because some people still sprinkle? Should we do away with the Lord's supper because we can't decide whether to use real wine or white grape juice?"

"You're changing the subject," Paul cautioned.

"I'm asking you to test your reasoning, your logic, your means of drawing conclusions, on other issues," said Pastor Smith.

"Jesus said that the gates of Hell would not prevail against the church," Paul said. "Would you have me believe that God would allow His gifts to be stolen from and then absent from the church from the first century until the 19th when they supposedly made their reappearance? Doesn't that kind of sound like Hell prevailing to you? History is silent about any gifts of the Spirit for hundreds of years."

"You're wrong," Pastor Smith said flat-out. "Augustine recorded healings. They're all over history, but the Christian church as a whole always attributed the accounts to heretics. And you have to remember, Pastor Corelli, that this was a church until the Reformation that considered the teaching of salvation by grace instead of works heresy."

And baptism by immersion, Alec thought.

But Pastor Smith didn't add that. He said, "Don't you think that the fundamental doctrine of

Christianity, salvation by grace, would be one that God wouldn't allow to be stolen and then absent?"

"It wasn't absent. There were always people who believed it."

"Yes. Right! And it's the same with the gifts of the Spirit. Hell did not prevail. A watered-down, compromising, blend into the world *Church* did."

"There are people who believe that they can play with poisonous snakes because of a verse in the Bible," Paul said. "Just because someone believes something, it doesn't make it biblically sound. That's why it's so important to consider the work scholars and theologians have done."

"All scholars and theologians have done is turn faith in Christ complicated." Pastor Smith grabbed a napkin and wiped up the creamer that had spilled from the opened but only partially used container he'd accidentally tipped. "If you gave the average person a copy of the Bible and told them to read it, they'd come away convinced that God works miracles. That's why all those 'simple' and 'uneducated' people in third world countries who are coming to Christ are also seeing all kinds of signs and wonders. But you never see any."

Paul leaned back, folded his arms across his stomach, and shook his head. "We're getting nowhere."

Fast, Alec thought, *and loudly.*

Suddenly, Paul leaned forward again. "Let's go to the Greek, Pastor Smith."

"Do you actually know Greek?"

* * *   .

As much as Vern Tompkins claimed to dislike winter, he sure enjoyed not having to get out of bed at 5:00 in the morning to open up his shop. He lived in a small trailer on the hillside right behind the shop, so it wasn't that it was such a chore to get there. It was simply that he preferred to sleep in, lounge around in his long-johns for a while with a newspaper crossword puzzle, and then dress at his leisure and head into town for his daily cup of coffee at his favorite café. He liked the waitresses there, and the company of the other retirees who frequented the place.

Today, though, the morning after Thanksgiving, a holiday Vern never had any use for, he only waved at the three men he usually sat with. His two pastor friends were sitting at a table near the window with a guy Vern had not seen in his shop. A guy whose veins were sticking out on his throat as he leaned forward to say something about 'Joel' and 'Paul' and the last days.

Vern had heard that phrase thrown around before—the last days. It was some religious concept. Something else he'd never had any use for. He almost decided to leave his pastor friends and Mr. *Let's Get So Emphatic That We Look A Little Psycho* to their conversation without stopping to say hello, but then Pastor Hale spotted him and raised his hand.

As Vern approached the table, the guy with the veins said, "We're in even last-er days than they were."

Pastor Corelli said something then, something that Vern understood even less than last-er days. Something about dispensations and authentication and the fact that nobody in the book of Revelation was performing miracles except the beast, his image, and the two witnesses, and that's the last-est last-er days.

"Where are all your Spirit -filled people then?" Pastor Corelli asked the other guy.

"They're gone," claimed Veins. And then he went off on something about the great tribulation.

So many —*ations*! It could give a guy a headache.

"How are you doing, Vern?" Pastor Hale asked, stiffly and loudly as he stood to shake Vern's hand.

Pastor Corelli stopped in the middle of what he was saying, looked uncomfortably between Alec and the guy with the veins, and then stood up to greet Vern as well. "Have a seat," he offered and then sat down and slid toward the window to make room for him.

"Thanks." Vern sat down.

"You don't ice fish?" Pastor Hale asked him.

"Nope."

"Vern," Pastor Corelli said, nodding toward the fourth man at the table, "this is Pastor Byron Smith."

"Pleasure," Vern said as he extended his hand, even though it wasn't that much of a pleasure. The man's mind was clearly still back in the conversation his arrival had interrupted. He smiled politely enough, but Vern doubted that he'd even heard his name.

Neither Pastor Smith nor Pastor Corelli spoke much to Vern while he sat there. They both sipped their coffee and stewed. That's what it looked like to Vern. But Alec made up for their silence with an ice fishing story from his youth, and Vern quickly forgot what the other two men had been talking about...though he'd not soon forget *how* they'd been talking about it. Arguing. A couple of pastors!

14

As always her desk was a mess, and also as always, Jenna Lachlan didn't have time to worry about it. She'd found the clippings and scribbled notes she needed, anyway. Interested in the now called 'rash' of vandalism against churches since the first occurrence, but unable to pursue it as a story beyond reporting the incidents when they happened and speculating about who might be behind it and why, Jenna thought she'd finally found an angle that would convince the people in ties to give her more room for it. Maybe as much room as its own couple of minutes on the evening news.

In general, people in Jenna's business didn't spend a lot of time with stories about the church or religion. Except, of course, when it engaged in hate speech, crimes, 'sin', and its increasingly frequent displays of intolerance. Some of the people at the station had privately applauded the vandals, whoever they were, and claimed that it was about time those 'oppressors' were given a dose of their own medicine.

Jenna did not hold to that opinion even though she held no love for churches, especially Christian. Hate was hate, no matter who it was aimed at, and she'd never applaud it. Whether the recipients deserved it or not.

Embracing the assertion that Christians *did* deserve any grief society could generate toward them—weren't they always the ones with their faces and Bibles in everyone else's business?—wouldn't be that much of a stretch for Jenna Lachlan. But trashing their buildings?

Burning them?

Jenna had been raised in a church. Sunday mornings. Sunday evenings. Wednesday nights. Week after week. Month after month. Year after year. She had seen her fair share and then some of the destructiveness of hoping and claiming to live one way when everything in you wanted to live another, and usually did. Guilt. Gossip. Hypocrisy. Repeated trips to the altar for rededication.

There was a time in her youth when Jenna had tried to 'live for God'. She had raised money for missions, youth group trips, women's ministries, vacation Bible schools, a new church parking lot. She had spent one Wednesday night a month on her knees with her forehead on a cold metal chair... supposedly in prayer. She had told people more than they'd ever asked to hear about Hell. She had decided not to wear make-up or tight clothes, and had given up her spot on the cheerleading squad because it certainly wouldn't please God to look down from Heaven and spy one of His daughters jumping around in only half a shirt and even less of a skirt. She had burned her secular music collection. She had read through her Bible in a year. Two years in a row. What it had come down to was about seven chapters a day, every day, for three hundred and sixty five days. Twice. She had actually enjoyed it, too, except Leviticus, Numbers, and that eternal Psalm. 119, was it?

She could no longer remember.

What she did remember was that it was never enough. No matter what she did. God, through her parents, her youth pastor, her pastor, her Christian friends, her own inner voice, always demanded more, better, higher, cleaner, lovelier, purer, deeper. More.

Jenna had gotten to a certain point in her pursuit of all that *more* when she realized that something was missing. Everything. Here she was, doing all the right stuff, and she was still empty inside. 'Living for God' wasn't making her any happier than living for herself had. In fact, it was making her miserable. So she'd put her tight clothes back on, quit going to church, moved into her own place, started working at a radio station which led to the job she had now, and gradually learned to tune out that part of her conscience that kept calling to her to go back, only for real this time to live *in* Him, not just *for* Him.

"Yeah, whatever," Jenna whispered to the folder in her hands. It irritated her, how near to her thinking that summons back could be when she gave it the slightest amount of room.

She wasn't at all interested in going back to church. But there were a couple of pastors she did want to chat with.

* * *

Bruce Finch despised hastily called board meetings. They stole his lunch hour. But more than that, it invariably meant that someone had a burr in his back pocket about something and wasn't going to rest until everyone else had a chance to sit on it too.

"Okay," he began, "most of us have to go back to work, so let's get this done." He looked at Marvin Klundt, the man who'd instigated the meeting. "What's on your mind?"

As if anyone needed to be told.

"Pastor Corelli has lost his focus," Marvin said. He was a big man, old, a member of the board of this church since before God created the earth. He'd learned to encapsulate. And to prefer it.

Many of the other men had not.

"He's spending too much time on this Christmas Eve service thing," one of them said.

"And with Pastor Hale," added another.

"I tried to get hold of him this morning about the children's church curriculum," a third complained, "and guess where he was?" He paused, but for effect only. Not long enough for anyone to actually answer. "With Pastor Hale at that other charismatic pastor's church."

"Pastor Smith?"

"The same."

"He's an…"

"I'm sure he was just helping him clean up."

"Why were you calling about children's church curriculum? Isn't that George Hammond's department?"

"Doesn't Pastor Corelli have today off on account of Thanksgiving?"

Bruce tapped his notepad with the tip of his pencil. He'd been getting grief from every front about Pastor Corelli lately, Raylene included. Like the proverbial dripping on a rainy day. Molly Avery's wedding which wasn't going to be a wedding now, and on and on and on. While he agreed with some of the observations about his pastor's shift in focus, he did not agree that it constituted a crime or a breach of his contract. Personally, Bruce thought the Christmas Eve service was a much needed endeavor. The fact that one of the men on this board had only been kept from insulting another Christian by someone else's interruption proved that much. And as to the supposed destructiveness of Pastor Corelli's close association with Alec Hale…Bruce suspected that none of the people whining about it had bothered to meet the man personally. As far as he'd been able to observe, and he had made it his business to not only meet the man but to spend some time with him, Pastor Hale was a man of genuine character and faith. True, he was off on his doctrine, but Bruce had no doubt that every Christian, upon arriving in Heaven and having some time to jaw about it with God, would discover plenty of 'offness' in his own life and persuasions. After all, if understanding God's Word and His hand in the lives of men was so easy and obvious, why didn't everyone understand it equally?

We will in Heaven, he thought. "I suppose you have some suggestions?" he said to Marvin.

"I think we should urge Paul to give Pastor Hale a deadline, for one," the older man answered. "A date when he has to be out of our building."

"To what end, Marv?" Bruce asked. "All that is going to accomplish is making Pastor Hale and his congregation uncomfortable here."

"That's exactly what it's meant to accomplish," Marvin said. "People resist change when they're comfortable. We don't want this to be an ongoing thing, do we?"

"They've already begun rebuilding," Bruce pointed out. "How would it look if we kicked them out before their new building was done? It would basically negate the fact that we'd shared our building with them at all."

"Everyone will understand," Marvin said. Then he laughed a little. "Maybe Pastor Smith would share *his* facility with Alec and his people."

"This church pays Paul Corelli," one of the other men said. Apparently, they had been wandering too far from the point to suit him. "His attention should be here. On this church. Not on some joint service that half of us aren't in favor of anyway. He should be at our church, if he's working today, to answer anyone's questions about the children's church curriculum or anything else, not out chumming around with a bunch of other pastors."

"Especially the pastors in question."

"You people really need to get lives," Pete Gress said. Then he stood up and collected his briefcase and coat. "Bruce, mark me as voting against any suggestions to give Pastor Hale a deadline. And mark me against any votes taken to do anything to discourage Paul from moving forward with the Christmas Eve service and giving it as much attention as he sees fit." He stepped away from the table. "I've got a life, thank you, and I'd rather be there than here." He started to walk away, but then turned back. "If you ask me, you are the ones who have lost your focus. My two kids have done nothing but grow in God since Paul and his family got here. The church is more active in reaching new people than it ever has been. The pew-sitters are actually talking about God after church now instead of football, lunch, or what the pastor did or didn't say right. Tithing is up. Attendance is up. Enthusiasm is up. The people are really glad to be helping Pastor Hale and his church, and they should be. It's only people like Molly Avery—and don't forget to look at her reasons—who are down."

Bruce watched the other men at the table watch Pete Gress leave. He'd never seen this group so completely speechless. It was singularly gratifying. Before they could regain their tongues, though, he said, "I don't think we'll be taking any votes today, gentlemen. If you are opposed to the Christmas Eve service, stay home. And if you must grumble about it, have the guts to do it to Paul's face instead of here behind his back." He pushed his chair back and got stiffly to his feet. As much as he wasn't in a hurry to get back to unloading trucks down at the depot, nothing looked better than escaping this meeting. "Call Alec Hale and go have coffee with him. I think you'll be surprised at how much you'll be finding yourselves liking the guy."

He heard a comment muttered behind him as he left the room, and a few chuckles about it, but he kept walking and didn't look back.

Next thing, he'll be wanting to open our board meetings in tongues.

Not likely.

* * *

Larry Quinn waited to hear Shayna's voice in the kitchen before picking up the phone. He'd been trying all morning to get hold of Alec, and his conversation with Shayna just now had only intensified his resolve.

"Some of the youth group kids were really slamming Pastor Hale Wednesday night," Shayna had confided. Larry had been unable to determine before his daughter remembered that she was needed in the kitchen whether she was troubled out of defensiveness for her pastor or out of irritation at him, but troubled she definitely was.

Just one more drop in what was rapidly becoming a downpour.

First it had been the worship leader. Then the youth leader. Then a concerned parent or two or three. Then the secretary. The drummer. One of the cell group leaders. And now his daughter.

Larry was used to people coming to him when they had concerns about Alec. It seemed to him sometimes that that, as elder, was all he was in the minds of everyone in the church *but* Alec. The guy you went to to grumble about the pastor. Larry didn't figure that he'd been called out of darkness just to be a sounding board for people who didn't have the backbone to deal with an offense scripturally. And he and Alec had an understanding. More than that, they had a friendship. So he always gave people two options. One, they could go talk to Alec themselves by the end of a week. Two, Larry would talk to him for them.

Stephanie answered the phone on the second ring.

"Is Alec home yet?" Larry asked her.

She laughed. "No, Larry. He and Paul are…"

"I know," he said. "At Pastor Smith's church."

"Sorry," Stephanie said. "What's wrong, Larry?"

"Oh, you know," he said. And he knew she did.

There was a pause before Stephanie said, "Alec knows people are talking. He's spending too much time on the Christmas Eve service. Too much time with Paul and other non-Spirit-led pastors. He's lost his freshness. His vision. He's quenching the Spirit." Another pause. "Does that pretty much sum it up?"

"Yup," Larry said. "Pretty much."

"I'll tell him you called," she said. Then, sincerely, she added, "Thanks, Larry. We appreciate you. Especially now."

He couldn't help wondering, as he hung up the

phone, if a guy on Paul Corelli's board was trying to get hold of *his* pastor this morning. Even though there were many differences between their two churches when it came to doctrine, he didn't doubt that they wouldn't have to compare notes when it came to the propensity of the inevitable loud few to disparage the men God had placed over them.

* * *

Instead of heading straight home after the board meeting, Marvin Klundt chose the less than scenic route through the town's industrial district. He needed some time to digest what had just happened.

Never before had he been so completely dismissed. Never.

Those two youngsters had a lot of nerve. A lot of it, all right. First Pete Gress, which did not surprise him so much. Pete tended to side with pastors during conflict. It was just his way. But Bruce Finch? Now that was hard to figure.

Give Alec Hale a call and go have coffee with him, indeed!

Marvin could think of several things he'd like to do when it came to Pastor Alec Hale, and sharing fishing stories on either side of a couple slices of pie was definitely not one of them.

The man had undermined him. He'd worked his way into their building and into their pastor's confidence, and now he was turning their board all topsy turvy.

Something had to be done. Soon. And if he

could get it done in time to put a serious damper on that ridiculous Christmas Eve service production, so much the better.

15

"Here's some tea, Dad."

Ed Cooper took the warm cup from his son and held it tightly. He was trembling, so it was difficult to keep the tea from spilling. He couldn't remember the last time he'd been this sick. Fever. Chills. Headache. Cough. He had a feeling he wouldn't be feeling like going anywhere in the morning, and he hated to call in sick. Good thing it was Friday. "Isn't tonight a coffeehouse night?" he asked Will.

"Yeah."

"You don't have to stay home."

"I might go for a little while," he said. "I want to talk to Jon about what we talked about this morning."

Ed nodded.

"But I'm going to stay until you're sleeping." Will took the cup from him and set it on the towel he'd placed on the coffee table. "Do you want me to turn on the TV? Should be just about time for the news."

"Sure." But he knew he wouldn't be able to concentrate on the news. He was having a hard time concentrating on anything at the moment except the fact that he'd never cared for Will when he was sick. He couldn't even remember his son being sick, though he was certain that he had to have been sick several times in the years since Sarah's death. Had he just sent Will up to his room? Had he ever taken his temperature? He couldn't remember. "Will?"

"Yeah, sir?"

"What did I do when you were sick?"

Will grinned. "You gave me whiskey."

"I gave—oh, Will, I'm…"

"Don't say it."

Ed shut his mouth. Will had to be exhausted of hearing apologies from him. Apologies he might still be struggling to believe.

"It worked most of the time," he said. "The whiskey."

"And when it didn't?"

"I got aspirin from the school nurse. She used to let me stay in her office because she couldn't call you." He straightened the towel on the coffee table. "She was always nice to me. Once I got older, I just took care of myself."

"I'm sorry, Will."

"I know."

Both of them looked at the television and the news played in front of them. Then a few commercials. Holiday greetings from local businesses, mostly.

For the first time since his wife's death, Ed

Cooper was looking forward to Christmas. He hadn't bought a tree because he figured Will was too old for that, but he had picked up a few gifts.

Something else he hadn't done in the past.

Something else he could apologize for if only he could summon the words to do it adequately.

Something else he'd have to give to Jesus, because he couldn't change what he had done or hadn't done in the past.

"Christmas actually means something this year," he said to Will.

"Yes, sir."

The news came on again. *With Christmas only two weeks away, many of us are feeling the squeeze of that all too familiar holiday stress...*

"Pastor Hale said we could have Christmas dinner with them," Will said.

"I know. He talked to me at church Sunday."

"Are we going to?"

"Would you like to?" Spending Christmas at home, just him and Will, was what Ed wanted. But he understood that Will might want something else.

"What if me and you just do something?" Will ventured quietly. "Go skiing, or something?"

Ed laughed until he had to lean forward coughing. "I don't ski," he said when he'd finally caught his breath.

"I thought maybe you had." Will shrugged and looked away from him. "I guess we could go to Pastor Hale's."

"What if you and me do something. Just not skiing."

"Really?"

Ed ached at the almost reluctant surprise in his son's voice and eyes. How many years had Will hoped that at Christmas, at least, his father would show him some kind of love? And how many years had he been disappointed?

All of them.

"We'll think of something, Will," he said. "Together. Okay?"

Will nodded. "Okay."

They turned their attention to the television again just in time for another barrage of holiday greetings and a wine commercial.

Ed stretched out on the couch and shut his eyes. They were burning. He thanked Will when he felt him add another blanket over him and would have fallen asleep right then except that the news was back on and some lady was talking about Pastor Hale and Pastor Corelli and their Christmas Eve service.

"...the mood among many members of Christian churches seems to be guarded this year," she was saying. Her over-precise enunciation made Ed wonder if her head wasn't as stuffed up as his was. "And it's no wonder, with the string of vandalism against their houses of worship."

Ed opened his eyes to see the file footage of the damage done to one of the churches, and the blackened parking lot where Pastor Hale's church used to stand.

"But two local pastors have taken it upon themselves to unite Christians for the holiday at a city-wide Christmas Eve service." The reporter went on to mention the arena where the event was to be held, the service time, and a contact name and number for anyone interested in participating. "So far," she said, "there seems to be a lack of interest, but organizers are hopeful that that will change as the day gets closer."

"We realize that there…"

"Hey, that's Pastor Corelli," Will said.

"Shh," Ed said.

"Sorry, sir."

"—many different churches out there who believe a lot of different things, but we are hoping to get together for a joyful time of celebration of one of the two major events on the Christian calendar."

Pastor Corelli's face on the screen was replaced by that of a rankled looking individual who said, "Celebrating Christmas at all in reference to God is a sham." He smiled, but still didn't look any happier. "Everyone knows that the actual birth of Christ did not take place in December and that it's only celebrated then because the early church tried to meld all its holy days in with the pagan celebrations of the culture around them."

"It will be interesting to see," the reporter, who was back on the screen again, said, "if the churches in town are really as one and the same as they must appear to be to whoever has been vandalizing them. John?"

"Thanks, Jenna. Mark will be in next with a look at our weather. He says you may want to take some precautions if you're planning to drive to your holiday destination."

Will pressed a button on the remote and the television went black. "I wonder where that lady dug that guy up."

"I don't know," Ed said. "I still don't see what the big deal is. I mean, we all agree that Jesus was born, right?"

* * *

The news and the sitcom afterwards continued to flash and blare in front of Raylene Finch, but she was no longer hearing or seeing the TV. Her mind had gotten stuck on that young red-haired woman's report. Her pastor's appearance. That guy who sounded more like a member of one of those cults who always put people on your doorstep than any real Christian protesting this or any celebration of Christmas and pontificating about the actual time of the birth of Christ. The reporter's last statement about the people who'd been vandalizing their churches.

"It will be interesting to see if the churches in town are really as one and the same as they must appear to be to whoever has been vandalizing them."

One and the same?

Not even close.

But, couldn't they be? More to the point, *shouldn't* they be? True, they would never interpret every scripture identically, they would certainly continue to worship differently, baptize in different names and at different times in a believer's life, evangelize or not, and feel that they, uniquely, had stumbled upon the most correct truths. But couldn't they still represent Christ as one? As the different individual members of one overall Church Body? Some congregations and denominations being the feet—doing most of the missionary and outreach work. Some congregations and denominations functioning as the hands—opening outreaches to the hungry and homeless and becoming involved in the political work, standing vocally against things like abortion, the redefinition of the family, liberalism in general. Some congregations and denominations focusing on prayer, worship, praise, intercession. Some congregations and denominations setting their goals on providing accurate understandings of the Bible and educating future church leaders. To the end that everything Christ would want and require from His Church would be getting accomplished.

Maybe if Christians would acknowledge one another on the basis of what they were doing right instead of always looking to peck away at what was wrong? Maybe if the cessationists would acknowledge that pentecostals did seem to be receiving more answers to prayer? And maybe if the pentecostals would acknowledge that cessationists tended to swing less on every new doctrinal fad that came along? Maybe if cessationists would take an honest look at the fact that the overwhelming majority of people getting saved in the world today were doing so in pentecostal churches? And maybe if pentecostals would take an honest look at the fact that most of the people standing visibly for holiness and the absolute authority of scripture were doing so from cessationist pulpits, ministries, universities, and seminaries?

Maybe.

But Raylene didn't plan to hold her breath.

It was much more fun to peck.

But if a person took the apostle Paul's comparison of Christ's church to a human body to its fullest extent, she'd have to ask herself how her physical body would or wouldn't function if her hand was always smacking her face, or her foot was always trying to kick her in the stomach—not that Raylene was that flexible anymore.

It would function with a lot of interruption and effort. But it could still function if the person, the brain at the heart of the body, was determined enough.

When it came to the Church as a body, Christ was Head over it. The strength behind it. The 'brains' of the operation. And there was no doubt, absolutely none, that He was determined to accomplish His will.

So maybe the diversity in the overall body of Christ could be used to His advantage, somehow. Maybe it already was, but the average human's ability to see more of the picture than the speck of it that constituted his life was hindering his cognizance of the fact that there even was a Big Picture.

Raylene glanced across the room at her husband. Hadn't he tried to get her to understand this, to understand his reasons for supporting Pastor Corelli and Pastor Hale in their efforts to organize this Christmas Eve service and to make the arrangement at their building work?

Yes. Bruce had tried.

But she'd been so focused, so obsessed, really, with Molly Avery's bitterness that she hadn't given his words a second though.

Until now.

The world should have the opportunity to see better than what Christians, as Christ's Church as a whole, had been showing it.

Raylene stood and went to the kitchen.

She'd used the phone to do a lot of damage to Pastor Corelli's reputation and to his vision. Now she was going to use it to repair that damage, at least as much as she could.

* * *

Becca Sullivan turned off her television and walked slowly past her dining room table to look through her sliding glass door at the side of the mountain, the snow, the night, and then at her own distorted reflection in the glass.

"So far there seems to be a lack of interest, but organizers are hopeful that that will change as the day gets closer," that reporter, Jenna Lachlan, had said.

Becca took a moment to examine her own attitude about the Christmas Eve service Pastor Hale and his friend Pastor Corelli were organizing. She'd been asked to sing on the worship team, but had declined. They were going to be doing a lot of hymns that she neither knew nor liked.

Now she had to wonder how she'd come to the conclusion that she didn't like the hymns since she didn't know them. She supposed it was because she never liked hymns. They were long, drawn out, full of antiquated language, and so complicated to read that a person had to work too hard just to keep from getting lost to even think about worshipping.

Recently, though, a friend had sent her the words to an 8th century Irish hymn in an email. The words had moved her. It was a prayer written twelve hundred years ago that she wished she was focused enough on Christ to claim as her own now.

But she wasn't and she knew it.

After receiving that email, Becca had picked up one of the hymnals from the pocket on the back of the pew in front of her in Pastor Corelli's sanctuary while Pastor Hale was preaching and had flipped through the pages, reading the words to certain hymns here and there. Some of them were silly and redundant, but many of them were like mini-sermons written to music. Full of truth and challenge. And somehow, when she skimmed the music after reading the words, it didn't look nearly as imposing or tedious as she'd always assumed it would be.

So here she was, this supposedly spiritual person, refusing to participate in something her pastor had asked her to consider because of conclusions drawn without the slightest effort to determine whether or not they had merit.

She wondered how many other conclusions she'd drawn that way. About people in her own church. About people in other churches and their means of worship. About the lost. About herself. About Christianity in general. About God, even.

She decided that first thing in the morning she'd call Pastor Hale and ask him if it was too late to sign up to sing on the worship team at the Christmas Eve service. If an obviously antagonistic-to-the-faith person like Jenna Lachlan had been able to cut through the static and hold up a standard—*one and the same*—then Becca Sullivan should at least try to do the same.

Because she loved the faith.

16

The weather and preparation for the holidays had been keeping the coffeehouse slow for the past several weeks, but Jon Hale barely noticed. His mind kept seeking out the future, thinking about the Christmas Eve service, imagining all the different ways it might turn out. He thought that he might even be more excited about it than his father was. Mostly because he was going to play his guitar as part of the worship team.

Many musicians from several different churches had met together the weekend before for their first rehearsal. The man in charge, a worship leader from a Baptist church, had already selected a song list and had come with very specific ideas in mind about how they would be performed. To Jon's way of thinking, the man's ideas were somewhat restrictive, but tolerable. All the other musicians apparently felt the same way. Anyway, nobody had complained.

The experience of playing in a gathering of so many talented people, most of them far more skilled on their instruments and knowledgeable about the structure of music than Jon, had humbled him a little and impressed him a lot. He was so excited about the next day's scheduled practice that he could hardly talk about anything else.

His friends had tolerated him up to this point, but he could see the beginnings of annoyance on a couple of their faces, most notably Zeke Hudson's. He decided he'd better change the subject. "Did you guys see the news?" he asked.

Justin shook his head. Kyra nodded. Zeke shrugged.

"Where's Will tonight?" Shayna asked.

Jon smiled. She must have seen his loss for words. But the smile didn't last long. "I don't know. He said he was going to be here."

"Are things going okay with him and his dad?" Justin asked after a moment.

"As far as I know."

"It's so good to see them together in church and stuff," Shayna said. "But I doubt that it's going as easily for them as that makes it look."

"Will should just get over it," Zeke said quietly. "He's lucky he's getting this chance with his dad."

Jon leaned back in his chair and studied Zeke. Though he and Zeke had spent a lot of time together, he still knew so little about him. Zeke was even worse than Will when it came to talking about his family. He knew better than to ask him anything now, in front of people, but he wished Zeke would open up to him more.

"There's Will," Kyra said. Then she leaned toward Shayna to whisper, "He's cute, isn't he?"

Jon watched Shayna shrug and smiled at her. He knew that she could not think about Will Cooper in such simple terms. Ever since that day that he and she had gone to invite Will to the coffeehouse and had found him drunk, she grew serious any time he was mentioned or came around. She was burdened for him. Something Jon understood and respected.

And shared.

He stood and went to the door, where Will was stomping the snow off his boots. "How are you doing?" he asked.

"I'm fine," he said. "It's Dad that's not so good."

It didn't escape Jon's notice, Will's calling his father *Dad*. This was a new thing. A good thing. But Jon kept his pleasure over it to himself. Will's father doing 'not so good' could mean any number of things, some of them scary. "What's up?" he asked Will.

"He's got the flu, or something. He's really sick."

Relieved first, concerned second, Jon said, "We'll have to go pray for him later."

"That would be good."

They walked together to the table and sat down.

"Did you guys get to see the news?" Will asked.

"Some of us." Jon had seen the report and it had made him angry. Dropping the opinion of that sour old man right in the middle of it as if what he had to say had anything to do with anything!

"They made it sound like nobody's going to the

service," Kyra said.

"Hardly anyone is," Shayna said.

"That's not true," said Justin. Then he reconsidered. "It's probably going to look like hardly anyone in that huge arena."

"Who cares?" Jon said.

Everyone looked at him as if he'd suddenly grown a third eye.

"Nice attitude, Hale," Zeke said. He stood and left the table.

Jon laughed. "I mean it. I'm tired of everyone whining about it. They're whining because they don't want to come. We're whining because they don't want to come. If people don't want to come, they can stay home and eat fruit cake. It'll be their loss. Not ours."

"Could be God's loss, too," Kyra said.

Jon looked straight at her. "God lose? All we can do, Kyra, is provide the event, invite people, and pray they'll come. The rest is up to them. Us worrying about it isn't going to change anything. God already knows who's going to be there." The door opened across the room, letting in some snow on a gust of icy air. Jon shivered. "And He knows who's not going to be there."

* * *

Paul and Rose Corelli had turned off the television and all the lamps but one and were enjoying the quiet evening. Jessica had gone to a school choir concert to cheer on one of her friends who'd be doing a solo, and Justin had gone to the coffeehouse with Jon, so they had the house to themselves. They'd agreed to not discuss the Christmas Eve service or church or Jessica's most recent outburst. Rose had steamed some shrimp and broccoli and had heated butter sauce, and had just sat down and handed Paul his plate when the phone began to ring.

"Don't answer it, hon," she said. He looked tired. Jessica's behavior was weighing heavily on him. It troubled her, too, of course, but Paul always downloaded more responsibility for his children's decisions than was healthy.

He smiled, kissed her forehead, handed his plate back to her, and pushed himself to his feet. "Rose," he said, "you know I have to."

"No, you don't. Let the machine get it. If it's urgent, you can pick it up. If it's just someone else calling to say they saw you on the news, you can call them to chat about it later." She smiled. He'd looked great on the news.

He sat beside her again. "All right. You're right."

"Of course I am." She held his plate toward him again just as the machine beeped and the caller started talking.

"Pastor Corelli," a female voice—and not a very pleasant one—said, "this is Molly Avery. I'm calling to tell you that I've decided to move in with Kent. I know it's wrong, and I don't want to do it, but you..."

Paul started to stand to go to the phone, but Rose stayed him with a firm hold on his wrist.

"...if you would have just married us all those ages ago, I wouldn't be in this situation. This is all your fault. All of it. You call yourself a pastor, and yet you were too wrapped up in your own power trip and all your little projects with that other pastor to show Kent the love of Christ. All you showed him was some rigid, unreasonable, man-made rule. And now I have to chose between losing him or living with him, and I'm not going to lose him and it's all your fault!" She hung up.

Rose placed her plate and Paul's on the coffee table. She shuddered at the nearness of her desire to hate that woman. "She's responsible for herself, Paul," she said.

He pulled away from her to lean forward. "Let's eat before it gets cold."

"Paul…"

"Please."

Knowing from experience that her husband wouldn't allow himself to talk about something like this until he'd had the time he needed to properly sort through it in his heart, Rose grabbed her plate, sat back, leaned against him while they ate, and chattered on about her hope to finish repainting the guest room before her parents arrived from New York for Christmas.

"I'll help you tomorrow," Paul promised.

A strange certainty, like a chill, whispered to her that he wouldn't. She hushed her mind, though.

Paul always kept his word to her.

* * *

Vern Tompkins stayed next to his wood stove for

several minutes. He'd thrown in a couple of pieces of cottonwood and he wanted to make sure they were going to burn. Cottonwood burned hot and long, but it could be stubborn about starting.

Sort of like Vern himself. He didn't like to try new things, but he did his research carefully and when he did decide to pursue something he immersed himself in it full force and forever. Like he had with fishing and his uncomplicated lifestyle.

Lately he'd been thinking about another decision. One he'd been staying ahead of until now but couldn't outrun forever. He'd seen another buddy's name in the obituaries that morning. It was only a matter of time before it would be his name there.

Both of his pastor friends had talked with him about that. Recently.

About being ready.

He knew that Alec and Paul believed different things. They'd told him so. And now he'd heard it on the evening news. But when it came to what they'd told him about dealing with the sin in his life and making himself ready to meet God, they had definitely been reading from the same book.

Everyone did things wrong. His pastor friends called that sin. Alec had told him that people are doing all kinds of mental gymnastics to deal with that fact. They're justifying it. Blaming it on someone else. Renaming it. Classifying it. But deep down inside, everyone knows that something is wrong. Something is missing. Peace, real peace, is always just out of reach no matter what measures people go to to try to grab hold of it.

Except for one.

Embracing what Christ had accomplished on the cross. The forgiveness of sins. The restoration of fellowship with God and His indwelling presence. Hope for eternity. The only real Life for right now.

"Religion is confusing," Paul had told him, "but Christ isn't. And He's what it all comes down to in the end. Whether or not we knew Him. I think God will give us some leeway when it comes to things like what we wear to church or the kinds of devotions we do and our interpretations of scripture, but there is no leeway when it comes to Christ. A person either knows Him or doesn't. If a person knows Him, he has Life. If a person doesn't..." He had shrugged and run his finger along his throat.

Vern had gotten the point.

But he didn't know what he had to do to request that Life from God. He'd always deliberately changed the subject on his pastor friends before they could get to that part of their spiel. The crying and praying part. He'd seen it on TV, he figured. He certainly didn't need to see it in his shop.

He remembered the crying and the praying part, but he couldn't remember what he had to say.

He knew that Paul and Alec were busy with the Christmas Eve thing coming up. He knew that he probably shouldn't bother them. But he also knew that he didn't want to wait anymore. He wanted Life.

His pastor friends wouldn't mind if he called them.

Maybe they'd even drive out tonight to talk with him.

* * *

As far as Stephanie Hale was concerned, she, at this moment, had everything she could possibly want. A Savior who loved her. Children who both loved Him. A new church building on the horizon. And the most wonderful husband in the world.

She leaned in closer to Alec. "Isn't it nice to have the place all to ourselves?"

He tightened his hold on her and kissed the top of her head. "Sure is."

He'd started a fire in the fireplace and they'd turned out all the lights to sit on the couch in front of it and do nothing but watch and enjoy it.

Very peaceful.

As perfect a moment as any on earth could be.

"Are you hungry?" she asked him.

"No."

"What are you thinking about?"

He smiled. "Absolutely nothing."

Knowing how much Alec needed to relax and do exactly that, Stephanie stopped asking him questions and allowed herself to savor simply being near him.

"We don't get enough times like this," she said quietly after a while.

"I know it," he said. "I'm sorry."

She pulled away from him so that she could see his face. "I didn't mean that…"

"I know what you meant," he said, pulling her back to himself. "Life is busy. And I don't have a nine to five kind of job."

She nodded. That's what she had meant.

"But we have right now," he said.

"Yes, we do."

The telephone rang.

Both of them laughed as Alec gently pushed Stephanie to her feet.

"Are you sure you want me to get it?" she asked him. But she was teasing, and didn't wait for a reply. She walked into the kitchen, flipped on the light, squinted at its brightness, and then picked up the phone. "Hales'."

"Uh...hello, ma'am. My name is Vern Tompkins. I was wondering if I might have a word with Pastor Hale?"

"Sure." She smiled. Alec had told her all about Vern Tompkins. "Just a minute." She brought the phone to Alec and nestled in beside him again as he spoke into the phone.

"Yeah, Vern," he said. "How're you doing? Is everything okay?" Pause. "Yeah, I remember." Another pause. A longer one. Alec leaned forward. "Vern, that's..." He nodded. "Yeah. Of course. I'll call Paul and we'll drive out." Pause. "Yes, I'm sure it's no problem." He stood, brought the phone back into the kitchen, and then hurried back out to Stephanie. "Steph," he said, "he wants Paul and I to pray with him to receive Christ!"

Tears pushed their way to Stephanie's eyes. She always cried when she heard that news. It was an involuntary thing. "Alec, that's wonderful. You've been praying for him for such a long time."

"Would you call Paul for me? Tell him I'm on my way?"

"Jon has the 4x4 at the coffeehouse," she reminded him. "He doesn't like to drive his truck on icy roads. You'll need the four wheel drive getting up that hill just before Vern's shop the way the roads are tonight."

"I'll appreciate it, anyway," he said. "Tell you what. I'll take your car, pick up Paul, and we'll run over to the coffeehouse to grab my outfit." He smiled. "Make you feel better?"

"Much."

Ten minutes later, after she'd called Paul, Stephanie Hale sat alone in front of the fire. Though she was happy about Vern's decision and about Alec's part in it, she couldn't help noticing how empty the house felt all of a sudden.

* * *

Cold air. Icy metal. A minor struggle with a couple of nuts that protested loosening. It was done.

Just like that.

And none too soon.

The Hale Mobile looked exactly as it always did, but it was all set to perform a little differently. When it did, the High And Mighty Hale family would understand that they'd been interfering with the wrong people.

People who were sick of being corrected.

People who were fed up with the holier than thou Hale attitude.

People who just wanted things to go back to the way they had been.

People who weren't afraid to keep sending a message.

A message that had thus far been ignored.

* * *

Paul slid into the front passenger seat, pulled the door shut, and buckled up. He felt cramped in Stephanie Hale's little car, but didn't say so. At least his knees fit under the glovebox. If they got in even the most minor of wrecks, Alec's kneecaps would be shattered.

Alec noticed Paul's gaze and must have known what he was thinking, as he seemed to so often. "We're not taking this all the way to Vern's," he said. "I'm going to pick up my outfit from Jon at the coffeehouse."

"Good," Paul said.

"I almost can't believe we're really going to pray with him," Alec said as they drove slowly along an icy side street.

"God is good," Paul said.

Alec glanced at him and then turned his attention back to the road. "Rough night?"

Paul supposed that if he sounded even half as stiff and numb as he felt, his tenseness would be obvious to Joe On The Street. And this was Alec. A guy who probably knew him as well as anyone, other than Rose. "Yeah," he said simply. "Had a call from Molly Avery."

"She was at your house on Thanksgiving?"

"That's the one."

"Don't let her get to you, Paul," Alec said. "You're making the right stand."

Rose had already told him that. Twice. Still, the assurance gave him no peace. "She called to tell me she's moving in with Kent, and that if I had shown him the love of Christ instead of…"

"You did show him the love of Christ."

"…sticking to my stand this wouldn't be happening."

"Give me a break." Alec pressed gently at the brake several times to get the car to stop at a snow-packed corner.

"That was great timing," Paul said.

"Huh?"

"You said 'Give me a break' just when you…oh, nevermind."

They laughed.

"Paul," Alec said when the light turned green and he began driving again, "what Molly Avery does is between her and God."

Paul nodded. He knew that. Besides, he shouldn't be allowing Molly Avery to steal his excitement about what they were on their way to do. Pray with Vern Tompkins for salvation! How awesome was that?

"I guess I'm just second-guessing, is all," he said to Alec. "I mean, how do I know for sure that the stand I took would have been God's stand? How do I know that it wasn't just mine? Maybe God would have married them and then they wouldn't be sinning now."

"They've been sinning all along, Paul."

"Right. Okay. But…"

"Listen," Alec said, "what does it say in 1 Corinthians 13:9?"

Paul sighed. "You're not thinking on turning this into a debate about the gifts of the Spirit, are you, because..." Paul felt Alec stiffen beside him and immediately regretted his words. This was why he'd quit talking to Rose about things that were troubling him until he'd had a chance to bring them to God. Alec Hale had never turned any of their conversations, even the ones about the Holy Spirit, into a debate about the gifts. He hadn't even joined in that day at the café when Pastor Smith had ambushed him. As it was, he felt as if he'd lost that conversation. How much worse would it have been if Alec had jumped in? "I'm sorry, Alec," he said. "I haven't had a chance to pray about this yet, and it's still bugging me."

"I'll leave you alone so you can pray on the way to Vern's."

Paul nodded. He'd definitely want to be rid of his attitude before he stepped into Vern's front room, and more importantly, into this most crucial event of his life. "What did you have in mind about 1 Corinthians 13:9?"

"It says that we only know in part. You made a stand with Molly and Kent that to the best of what you can discern is scriptural. God knows that. He knows that we don't have the complete knowledge that He has."

1 Corinthians 13:9-10 had been at the heart of many of the books he'd read and many of the classes he'd attended at seminary, but he'd never heard

anyone use it like that. To Paul's way of thinking, and to the way of thinking of every cessationist Paul had ever known or heard or read, this scripture was basically the crux of their argument against the present day manifestations of the gifts of the Holy Spirit.

"For we know in part, and we prophesy in part. But when the perfect comes, the partial will come to an end."

The church had the Bible now, God's written Word, for instruction, guidance, teaching, and direction. It no longer needed the supernatural intervention and completely visible leading of the Holy Spirit. So that which was in part—prophecy—could be done away with.

"Alec," he said, "we have the Word of God now. It has in it the answer to everything."

"No argument there."

"It's either wrong or right to marry a Christian to a non-Christian."

"Again, no argument."

He felt frustration tugging at the back of his neck. "So, what's your point? We don't have to know in part anymore. We have the Word."

"All right," Alec said. "Let me ask you something about that. What do the next few verses underneath 1 Corinthians 13:9-10 say?"

Paul couldn't remember.

So Alec told him. "It says, *When I was a child, I spoke like a child, I thought like a child, I reasoned like a child. When I became a man, I put aside childish things. For now we see indistinctly, as in a mirror, but then face to face. Now I know in part, but then I will know fully, as I am fully known.*" He stayed quiet a moment. "Paul, I know that you believe that the 'when the perfect comes' clause is referring to the written Word. But how can you look at those next few verses and draw that conclusion? It doesn't say we'll have the *potential* or the *tool* to know as fully as we are known, it says that whenever whatever 'the perfect' is comes, we *will* know fully, as we are known." He shrugged. "We're not there yet. You and I both have the Bible. We both read it. We both love it. We both look to it for every answer. And yet, you and I don't see eye to eye. How can that be, if the Bible is 'the perfect' that's coming? It seems to me that we're still in the *knowing in part* stage."

"The Greek is neuter, there, Alec, not masculine. So 'the perfect' can not be referring to Christ."

"I understand that," Alec said. "What about *Word* in John 1:1? Is that masculine or neuter?"

In the beginning was the Word, and the Word was with God, and the Word was God.

The Word. Jesus Christ.

He'd have to look into that.

Because if 'the perfect' did not refer to the Bible or the Church or anything else that had appeared yet, then…

Alec pulled the car in beside his 4x4 in the coffeehouse parking lot and killed the engine. He pushed open his door and struggled to swing his legs around and out. "If it's any comfort, Paul, I won't marry a Christian to a non-Christian, either."

* * *

Shayna Quinn nudged Jon when she saw his father enter the coffeehouse with Pastor Corelli. Then she looked at Will Cooper. "Pastor Hale is going to be so excited that you and your dad want to be water baptized."

"Looks like he's already pretty excited about something," Will said.

Shayna noted Pastor Hale's smile and his quick and purposeful strides. Since she'd seldom seen him looking bored, though, she said, "Well, whatever it is, your news is going to top it for sure."

But then Pastor Hale was at their table trading car keys with Jon, hurriedly explaining about some guy named Vern who was wanting to give his life to Christ, *tonight,* and leaving again with Pastor Corelli.

Shayna felt a little embarrassed as she leaned toward Will Cooper again. "Well," she said, "it'll be his best news tomorrow."

17

"Louise? This is Raylene. Have you got a few minutes?"

When Louise said that she did have a few minutes, Raylene clutched the receiver and started talking. The fact that this was her fourth phone call softened the difficulty and bitterness of the task not at all. Admitting you'd been a jerk, and even worse had ignored scripture, was quite a sour bite to swallow. Especially aloud. To people who ordinarily looked up to you. And especially when none of those people understood.

"Honey," Louise said reassuringly when Raylene had finished, "you didn't do anything wrong. We can't just sit back and tolerate everything for the sake of peace."

"I'm not saying we should. I'm…"

"Pastor Corelli was wrong to not marry Molly and Kent. It's so legalistic. And, I mean, hasn't he read the scripture about the believing wife saving her husband?" She huffed. "Anyway, he might have seen the situation more clearly if he hadn't been so preoccupied with all his other little projects."

"I think he told Molly he wouldn't do the wedding before he and Pastor Hale started working together on the Christmas Eve service or sharing our building or anything, Louise," Raylene said, the realization sickening her. How flimsily they'd pieced together the 'facts' and their offenses. "It's just his stand. Anyway, even if he is wrong, it doesn't make it right for me or you or…"

"He…"

"…anyone else to go around tearing him apart behind his back."

As Raylene listened to another barrage of whiny disbelief from Louise, she thought back to a Bible study their former pastor's wife had led out of the book of Galatians. She couldn't bring to mind the exact verse, but had no trouble boiling it down to its reality in her present situation.

All the law could be summed up in one phrase: *You shall love your neighbor as yourself.* And especially those of the household of faith, she seemed to remember reading. *But if you bite and devour one another, watch out, you'll be consumed by one another.*

"Louise," she said, interrupting her friend, "I've still got a couple of phone calls to make. I'll call you tomorrow, okay?" Then she hung up without waiting for Louise's reply.

* * *

Knowing that he should feel like the happiest guy in the world only added to Kent Sherman's restlessness. He'd won his argument with Molly. She'd agreed to move in with him. He was in the position to get everything he wanted without making the slightest commitment. He now knew he was more important to Molly than her religion and her God. And she looked absolutely to-die-for in the lacy little mint green thing she'd just slipped into.

And yet her nearness disgusted him.

Because *The Chase* was over?

He didn't think so. He'd never really had to chase Molly. She'd pretty much given herself to him right from the start.

Because she'd been temperamental all evening?

No. Molly tended to be that way. He'd taught himself early on in their relationship to not be bothered by it.

A lot of possible explanations for his jumbled emotions criss-crossed back and forth across his mind, but one persistent thought lay still and softly behind all of them.

God.

Kent was repulsed by Molly—no, by their situation—because of God.

Though he tried to ignore the thought because he didn't even believe in God, it kept its quiet vigil and he told Molly he needed to be alone.

She sulked for a moment, but then shrugged

and went into the other room, slamming the door behind her.

Pastor Hale had told Kent at Thanksgiving dinner about a spiritual void that was supposedly inside every human being. A need. A hunger. An emptiness. A void that existed because we were created to be in fellowship with God but had separated ourselves from that fellowship through sin. People spent their lives trying to fill that void, that hole, with relationships, money, material gain, status, achievement, drugs, their careers, their hobbies, their causes, and even their religions. But the only thing that could truly fill it, according to Pastor Hale, was God. God Himself.

Kent had listened to Pastor Hale and had even given his words some thought in the days immediately following their conversation. But his mind had always brought him back to Molly for a conclusion, a reprieve.

She knew God, and she was one of the most miserable and unhappy people Kent knew.

Of course, she was *sinning*, wasn't she? Separating herself from God again. Willingly. Willfully. Even Kent had to acknowledge that if there was a God and you had been close to Him, being apart from Him again, even just a little bit, would be disquieting.

Miserable.

Kent supposed that if he were to be totally honest with himself—and shouldn't he be?—he'd have to admit that there had always been an emptiness (that was the perfect word for it, though he'd never been able to put a finger on it before) inside him. It could be filled for a while but never permanently. He could purchase that new car or work toward that new goal or catch that new woman, but the satisfaction of it always faded.

Always.

He'd never been a person to get behind a cause, and he'd never tried religion. And he didn't necessarily want to start now.

But what if Pastor Hale was right about that hole inside him and about God's ability to fill it? To *really* fill it.

Maybe he'd call Pastor Hale in the morning. Maybe they could talk. Maybe he could come to terms with that quiet, still prodding at the back of his thoughts.

Maybe.

One thing was for sure. He wasn't going to go to Molly tonight.

* * *

Alec Hale drove slowly along the quiet residential street that would bring him to the westbound Interstate entry ramp. He wasn't talking, because he'd promised Paul the time on the way to Vern's to pray. The heater was blowing full force, but had so far failed to take the edge off the cold. He wished he had thought to grab his gloves.

As he drove, he prayed silently. For Vern. For Jon, Justin, Zeke, Will, and the others he'd seen at the coffeehouse. For Paul. Boy, he knew how it felt to be in doubt about a stand you'd taken. How depleting it could be. Especially when it had resulted in an outright accusation. He also knew, though, that Molly Avery and her boyfriend were making, and were accountable for, their own choices. He prayed for them, too. And then for Stephanie. The Christmas Eve service.

He nudged the gearshift as he increased his speed to enter the Interstate. There wasn't a lot of traffic but the roads were icy, so his hands tightened instinctively on the wheel.

The ride turned from smooth to rough and then loud as metal scraped against pavement and threw up sparks. Alec didn't know what was happening except that he'd lost control of his vehicle. He couldn't remember whether he was supposed to steer into or away from a spin and when he turned his head to look out his side window, all he saw was light.

Bright, loud light.

* * *

Rudy "Tallman" Hansen sat completely still for a moment, trying to determine whether or not he was in pain. He wasn't, except for one long gash that ran across the back of his right hand. His windshield had shattered, spraying glass everywhere. But other than that, the inside of his cab seemed to be pretty much in tact.

That wouldn't be the case with the car he'd hit. He knew that. He couldn't even see it now, even though his headlights were still beaming out. All he could see was the dented guardrail and the tree-spotted canyon wall beyond it. In between the two...nothing but shadow.

Glass crunched somewhere beneath his feet as he shifted his bulk to reach his CB.

He'd been hauling trailers for fifteen years, and he'd never seen anything like this. The guy's wheel had come off the axle. Right in front of him. Leaving Rudy no time to react. Nowhere to go but into him.

18

That place just between wakefulness and sleep. Where you can hear everyone and everything around you, but wouldn't be surprised by the appearance of someone who'd died when you were a child. Where voices were muffled, words seldom made sense, and you couldn't see clearly even though you were sure you'd opened your eyes.

That's where Paul Corelli felt trapped. Flashing lights. Strong hands. Voices. Faces. Cold. Pain. Numbness. Sleep. Rose.

She was asking him to do something, but he couldn't understand.

"Paul, open your eyes."

They are open.

But they must not have been, because Rose didn't stop asking.

More voices.

A cold hand over his.

* * *

Elise Hale stared down at Pastor Corelli. His bruised hand felt hot against hers. She glanced over her shoulder, hoping to borrow some courage from Mrs. Corelli because hers had run empty. But Mrs. Corelli had gone out to the hallway. Elise could see her through the blinds, hugging her mother.

Just as well. If Mrs. Corelli had any courage to spare, Mom needed it more than anyone.

She looked back at Pastor Corelli.

"You're lucky you're unconscious," she said, and then startled. Not at her voice so much as at its intrusion on the silence in the room.

She preferred the silence.

Pastor Corelli had been unconscious for a day and a half. There had been so much noise during that time. The phone call. The rush to the hospital. Doctors. Police. People coming to pray and wish well and console and comfort and grieve and help.

Elise shut her eyes and concentrated on breathing.

Just breathing.

"Dad's dead," she whispered to Pastor Corelli. She wondered if he knew that. If he knew what had happened. The police said that the accident had happened fast. And that it might not have been an accident. Something about the wheel that had come off and signs that it may have been tampered with. She wondered what the last moments of her father's life had been like, and if Pastor Corelli would be able to tell her what he'd said, if anything, before…

She shut her eyes again.

You have to breathe.

Elise wasn't sure how long she stayed beside Pastor Corelli before her mother came in to get her. She wasn't sure why she'd gone in in the first place. She wasn't sure where her mother wanted her to be instead. And she wasn't sure she knew what to say when Mrs. Corelli whispered, "Oh, honey, I'm so sorry," and hugged her.

At that moment, the only thing Elise Hale felt sure of was that she'd never allow herself to feel sure of anything again.

* * *

"You really ought to go home," Rose said quietly to Stephanie as they walked along one of the tens of hospital hallways they'd all become too familiar with. This one led to the cafeteria. "You're exhausted, and being here…"

"Is what Alec would want me to do," she said. "I can't leave until there's some word on Paul."

Rose stopped walking, placed her hands on Stephanie's shoulders, and turned her to face her. She felt tears at her eyes, but refused them. She would not cry in front of Stephanie Hale. Not about Paul, anyway. He was alive. "Honey," she said, "nobody knows how long it'll be before he wakes up." She released Stephanie's shoulders and started walking again. "It could be hours or days or weeks. I don't expect you to stay here."

Some friends of Elise's met them in the hallway. Hugs and tears were followed by a quick recital of information and then the three girls, with Elise in the middle looking tiny and fragile, left.

Rose waited a moment and then placed her hand at Stephanie's elbow to get her moving again. They walked the rest of the way to the cafeteria without speaking. They chose food without interest. They appreciated the lack of eye contact or comment from the girl at the cash register. They found a table. They prayed silently. They pushed more food around than they ate.

"Why would someone want to hurt us?" Stephanie asked, not looking up from her mashed potatoes.

Rose was sure she wasn't expected to answer. But she said, "I'm sure the person who loosened the lug nuts, if that's what happened, didn't intend for..."

"I know."

Rose didn't finish her sentence. Stephanie looked ready to shatter. Besides, it really didn't matter what anyone had *intended,* did it? All that mattered was what *was.* "You should go home, Stephanie."

Stephanie shook her head and waved her hand over her food as if she could shoo her feelings aside like a pesky fly. "I don't want to go home."

"I understand," Rose admitted quietly. She wouldn't want to go to her house, either, if Paul was gone. Not right away. But she wouldn't want to stay at the hospital where he'd died, either, and she didn't want Stephanie Hale feeling any obligations on account of their husbands' friendship or on account of their being in the car together or on account of feeling responsible, somehow, because their vehicle had been the target of someone's ill-will and tampering and Paul had been an innocent tag-along. But she didn't know how to say what she was feeling, and, more than that, she was well aware that her feelings at the moment could not be trusted. "Honey," she said, "eat."

Stephanie nodded and obeyed.

"Good," Rose said. "Take another bite."

Stephanie did. Then she smiled. "You, too, Rose."

Rose grimaced and forced in a mouthful of lasagna. *Nasty.* And it had nothing to do with the unavailability of genuine Italian products in western Montana.

"Is Justin with Paul?" Stephanie asked.

"Yes."

"He's got to pull through, Rose."

Rose took another bite of lasagna. Then another. And another. Quickly, until her mouth was full. She took some water to help in swallowing, wiped at her mouth with her napkin, and then pushed her plate forward. Enough. She was only eating so she wouldn't cry. But it was disgusting to eat like that, and the tears were coming anyway. "I'm sorry," she said to Stephanie.

"What on earth for?" Stephanie reached across the table and grabbed her hands. She was crying, too.

Rose didn't mark the time they spent there grieving. But they both finished at about the same moment. Neither of them said so, but Rose knew it had been a relief for both of them. Yes, their circumstances were different, but both of them were suffering. Trying to hide their true feelings from one another, even if to protect each other, had only exacerbated things.

And things were already awful enough.

"You should get back to Paul." Stephanie stood and took in a long breath. "And I should go find Jon. He's around here somewhere with Will."

Standing, too, Rose nodded.

"I'll walk you back up."

As they approached the elevators, a tall older man stepped toward them, quietly calling their names.

"Mrs. Corelli? Mrs. Hale? Justin told me I'd find you here."

Expecting the man to identify himself as another detective or a reporter or one of the many pastor acquaintances of one of their husbands, Rose stiffened her shoulders and forced a polite smile.

The man took gentle hold of Rose's hand. "I'm Vern Tompkins," he said slowly. "It, uh, it was me your husbands were coming to see the other night."

Rose watched as Stephanie grabbed the man's big hand in both of her small ones and smiled at him. The smile was genuine, Rose was sure. And accepting.

It clearly made Mr. Tompkins uncomfortable.

"Mrs. Hale," he said, "I would have come before now but I only just heard about the accident on the news this morning." He shook his head. "I can't believe…uh…I…"

"Alec was so happy about going to go see you, Mr. Tompkins," Stephanie said.

"Yeah, well, he should have stayed home."

"No." Stephanie looked intently up at the man as her hold on his hand tightened. "No. Nothing happens outside of God's reach, Mr. Tompkins. Somehow, some way, He's got something He can do with all this to make it fit."

"I don't see how," the big man said.

"I don't either, right now," Stephanie admitted. "But I do know Him. And I've seen Him do it before. In situations that seemed just as irredeemable as this one. Redeeming. That's His business, and He's good at it."

Suddenly Rose remembered why Paul and Alec had been going to see Vern Tompkins Friday night. And just as suddenly, an inexplicable steadiness hushed all the noise in her mind except for one thought.

Finish.

For a moment, Rose debated it.

Here? Now? Stephanie's not going to be up for that. I'm not up for that. For all I know, Mr. Tompkins has decided he doesn't want to know a God who would allow something like this to happen.

But the thought held out.

And Rose obeyed it.

She and Stephanie.

Apparently, Mr. Tompkins recognized that a hospital hallway was as good a place as any to repent of his sin and invite Christ to indwell him as Lord and Savior. Maybe a better place than many. And, apparently, the events of the previous day and a half had only cemented his realization of his need to do so.

When the three of them finished praying, the elevator doors slid open in front of them and they stepped inside.

It was time to get back to Paul.

* * *

Bruce and Raylene Finch, along with Larry and Robyn Quinn, stood at the entryway doors of their church while people quietly left the first service and then began to arrive for the second. Nearly everyone had heard about the accident already, but the two couples had agreed to meet between the two services to answer questions, offer encouragement—not that they had much of it to offer, and to present a united front to both congregations.

Understandably, Larry and Robyn and the rest of Alec Hale's people were significantly more distraught and in need of commiseration than Pastor Corelli's people.

Bruce tried to step out boldly with words of faith, support, and the overused and trite consolation that "God is in control," but he felt as if his efforts were hollow. Not that Alec's people didn't respond kindly and appreciatively to him. They did. It was just…what do you say to people whose pastor and friend had been so uselessly, violently, and unexpectedly stolen from them?

Fortunately for Bruce, and for Larry and Robyn, Raylene came through. She embraced people who needed embracing and upheld those less demonstrative ones with quieter proofs of her concern. A touch at the elbow. A slight squeeze of the hand. She seemed to know which person needed which type of comfort, and she offered it absolutely and individually.

Bruce guessed that she was in that not-daring-to-think mode of hers. Not taking time to second-guess herself or her perception. Trusting God to show Himself through her.

And He was.

As annoying as Raylene's apparent impulsiveness and lack of fear about sharing her opinion could sometimes be, it was—and always had been—a shining asset in situations like this. A saving grace.

"We don't have those answers right now, baby" she was saying to a sobbing teenager who was asking her why anyone would want to harm a pastor and why God had allowed them to succeed and what they were going to do now and how God was going to work good out of this like He promises. "The only answer we do have is that God knows all the answers, and in His time, we will, too. It may not be till we get to Heaven, so all we can do now is take confidence in the fact that He does know. Do you think you can do that?"

Bruce watched as the girl nodded, clung to his wife for a couple moments longer, and then silently walked away.

This was wrong. All of it. Why *had* God allowed such a seemingly irredeemable thing to happen? What good could possibly come of Alec Hale's death and Paul's as-yet-to-be-determined injuries? Who would intentionally tamper with someone's car, especially in the middle of winter? And why?

Bruce didn't have the answers. He couldn't even imagine any. And unlike his wife, he was having a hard time being content with not allowing himself to need them.

* * *

Will Cooper sat stiffly beside Shayna Quinn and her family near the front of the absolutely silent church. There had been no music before the service. No worship. No opening prayer. It seemed as if nobody had thought about what would be done once the sanctuary had filled. Finally, though, Shayna's father made his way to the front and stepped to the pulpit. Will heard the man's quiet words, he was sure of it, but he failed to be able to grasp them or to commit them to memory or even to keep up with them. It was as if his brain had gone hollow and everything was just sliding through except for the smothering and paralyzing fact of Pastor Hale's death.

He had just seen the man last night. In fact it occurred to Will with a pain he could taste that he had been among the last to see him alive.

He thought of his friend Jon and of his mother and sister still at the hospital with the Corellis. Jon had been there for Will. Strong. Competent. Committed. Now it was Jon who was going to need someone to be there for him, and it seemed to Will that Jon had already decided that Will was going to be the one. Jon had called Will to come to the hospital. Jon had asked him to walk around with him long after the doctors had brought in the word that there was nothing they'd been able to do for Pastor Hale. And Jon was the only reason Will was sitting in church.

"Go see Dad's people for me, Will," Jon had said to him. "I want to know how they are, but Mom wants me to stay here with her. Will you go? Tell them why we're not there?"

"They'll know why you guys aren't there," Will had assured his friend, and then he had driven alone to church.

And now he was sitting among two hundred or more people, Jon's father's people, who all seemed to be stammering in the same flood of numb-emotion as he was. Some were crying, but most just sat. Listening to Mr. Quinn. Feeling more questions than answers or assurances.

Why would God allow this?

Was it true that someone had tampered with the Hales' vehicle? If so, who? And why?

What would happen to the church?

Would Mrs. Hale, Jon, and Elise be okay?

Had Pastor Hale suffered?

Will shifted on the hard wooden pew. He felt as if he owed his life to Pastor Hale. His new chance at a life with his father. His life in Christ. Maybe even his physical life. And now the man was gone.

Taken away.

Will knew without doubt that Pastor Hale was with God now, and that even if he had suffered in the accident, he wasn't suffering now. This knowing offered some comfort. Some stability. Some peace.

The only peace.

This was the one thing Will had been able to say to Jon through the long long hours of the previous night.

Your dad is with God now, Jon.

Jon knew that already, of course, but he seemed to appreciate Will's saying it again and again. He seemed to need to hear it out loud. From someone outside of himself.

Will was glad to have been there for his friend in that small way, but he was no fool. Jon was going to need a lot more in the days to come and Will wasn't sure he was up to the task. He didn't know the Bible yet. He hadn't learned to pray the way he'd heard all the other kids pray at the coffeehouse and the way he'd heard Pastor Hale pray. He wasn't particularly good with words or with knowing when to say them or when to stay silent.

But up to the task or not, Will Cooper was determined to be there for Jon even when he didn't know what to do or say.

Jon was going to be lost without his father.

When Mr. Quinn finished speaking and people slowly and quietly began to leave, Will gently embraced Shayna, told her he'd see her later at the hospital, and left the church.

He'd go back to the hospital after a while.

He needed to go check on his father first. Wanted to. To see if he was feeling better. To see if he needed anything.

To hear his voice.

19

Pastor Paul Corelli stared through his window at snow dusted cars and mounds of snow beside shoveled sidewalks all along the side streets heading to his house. Rose was driving and seemed to know that he needed to think. She stayed quiet, even though he knew she was excited to be bringing him home after his long hospital stay.

He had missed Alec's funeral. He had awakened to find out that his closest friend in the world except Rose hadn't survived the accident, and that he'd remained unconscious through and past the funeral and into days in which others had already begun giving and receiving comfort and settling into numb but necessary states of acceptance.

Well Paul was not numb. Not even close. And acceptance was the farthest thing from his mind and heart.

He remembered flashes of the accident. The

light. The horn. Spraying glass. Cold. He remembered thinking that he and Alec couldn't possibly survive once he'd pieced the information of his panicked senses into a coherent thought.

A semi is ramming full speed into us!

So why had he survived?

When Alec hadn't?

When neither of them should have?

Why had he been able to walk out of the hospital with only a broken left arm, a couple broken ribs, and one jagged stitched together gash along the left side of his head?

Paul knew that he should be thanking God that he had survived and especially that he'd survived with minimal injuries. That he wasn't paralyzed. That he hadn't lost his memory or his hearing or his eyesight. Paul knew that he shouldn't be feeling like God made a mistake, somehow…that He'd accidentally taken the wrong guy, the better guy, home.

He knew all that.

And he knew he was being foolish and undisciplined to not direct his emotions more forcefully in the direction he knew they'd go eventually.

That numb and necessary state of acceptance. Maybe even as far as peace.

Paul knew that God is sovereign. Able to author good out of even the most apparently irredeemable situation. Full of grace. He knew the scriptures. The promises.

The truth.

And yet he felt so cold on the inside. As cold as all those mounds of snow he was passing.

"How many days till Christmas?" he asked Rose because he began to feel suffocated by the silence between them. Or was it by the noise in his own head? Either way, he needed the interruption of voices.

"Three," she answered.

"I know I've asked you that before," he apologized. "I'm having a hard time keeping track."

"That's all right," she said, turning her head to quickly smile at him.

"The Christmas Eve service." Paul kept looking at her even after she'd turned her attention back to the road. He hadn't asked about the service, and it seemed to him that people had kept deliberately away from the subject during their visits with him. "They've canceled it, I suppose?"

"No," Rose said. She pulled the car into their garage but left it running. For the heat, Paul was sure. "Paul," she said as she turned in her seat to look more directly at him, "it has been the most incredible thing. I told you they think someone loosened the lug nuts on Alec's wheel?"

Paul nodded.

"That's been all over the news. That Lachlan woman seems to be obsessed with the story."

"The *story*?" Paul could not believe that his friend's death in an accident that apparently was no accident had so quickly been reduced to nothing more than a *story* in people's minds. In his wife's mind.

Rose reached across the gearshift between them and tightly squeezed his hand. "I'm sorry," she said quietly.

And Paul knew that she was.

"It's just hard to put words to some of this," she said. "That's all. We're all doing the best we can."

Now it was Paul's turn to apologize.

"Anyway," Rose said, still holding tightly to his hand, "she mentions the accident nearly every day on the news. 'Still no clues as to who tampered with Pastor Alec Hale's vehicle or why' she'll say. And she's done interviews with people who know you and Alec. With some of the people who are participating in the Christmas Eve service." Rose grinned and shook her head. "She's flat out allowed people to share the true and complete meaning of Christmas in her pieces, right there on the evening news!"

"Sounds like a real open door," Paul said too quietly, not sure whether he should feel grateful to God for this one bit of light in the whole darkness of the situation or angry at Him for allowing the darkness in the first place.

Both, maybe. Or neither.

Rose didn't leave him time to decide. "Pastors from all over the state have called Stephanie, Paul. They want to support Alec's vision for unity, even though he's gone now, by bringing a couple car loads or van loads or busloads of their people to the Christmas Eve service." She smiled. "Even most of those pastors you called way back when you wanted to start your pastors prayer group have said they'd bring people. Pastor Stoltz. Pastor Pearson. Even Pastor Byron Smith."

Paul shuddered at his memory of the man, but then smiled. "That was Alec's dream."

"I know," Rose said. "And I'm sure he's seeing it happen."

Paul nodded. He was sure of that too. Even though a small part of him begged to be cynical—*all those pastors who Rose had mentioned by name had thought that Alec's idea was crazy, irresponsible, a waste of time when he was alive and several of them had told him so to his face, but now all of a sudden because of guilt or shame or some kind of warped sense of social correctness they think it's the right thing to do because someone had apparently killed Alec over it?*—the greater part of him, the stronger part, chose to be thankful. Maybe their hearts had finally softened. Maybe the running theory that someone was so opposed to Alec's plan that they'd mess with his vehicle in the middle of winter had awakened them to the fact that disunity in the Body of Christ really could be a harmful thing.

Of course, Paul wasn't sure that he bought that theory. It could have been a teenaged prank. Hadn't Alec's son actually had the vehicle? At that Christian coffeehouse? It was a change of plans that had placed Alec behind the wheel. Maybe the people responsible for all the church vandalisms had messed with the car. For all anyone really knew, it could have been nothing more than a random act by some wacko environmentalist who figured he'd get one more of those evil SUVs off the road for a while.

Who knew?

Nobody, Paul realized, but God and the person who had knelt beside Alec's vehicle on that cold night.

* * *

"What are they doing out there?" Jessica Corelli whispered to her brother. "They pulled into the driveway ten minutes ago."

Justin opened his mouth to answer her or more probably to tell her to be quiet, but was hushed by the sound of the door opening into the kitchen.

Jessica couldn't help smiling. Her father was finally home. He was well again…well, as well as could be expected. Even better. The family room was full of people who had come to welcome him. Mrs. Hale and Jon and Elise. Kyra Gress and her family. Other people from their church. And other people from Pastor Hale's church.

Everyone knew that her father probably wouldn't feel much like celebrating, and they didn't either. They hadn't hung streamers or blown up balloons or ordered in a cake. They'd just come. To welcome him home. To let him know they were glad he was okay.

To be there for him.

To support him.

To grieve with him.

Jessica glanced across the room at Jon and Elise. She still cried every time she let herself really think about them. She could not imagine losing her father. She wondered if they resented her when they looked across the room at her because her father was coming home today and theirs never would be. Never could.

They didn't act like they resented her.

It was just that she wondered.

Maybe because she'd resent them if the situation were reversed?

Maybe.

She shoved those thoughts away as her mother led her father into the den.

They were all out in the open of the room and nobody shouted *surprise* and yet her father looked genuinely stunned to see so many people. Tears piled in the corners of his eyes when he looked at Mrs. Hale.

Jessica was proud of him for not being embarrassed about them.

Tears came to her own eyes as she recalled how angry she had been at him when he wouldn't allow her to try out for that play at the community theater. That whole incident seemed now to have happened in a different lifetime. Before the accident. Before Pastor Hale's death. Before the hours and days of waiting for her father to wake up. Before she realized how blessed she was to have a father who cared enough about her to care about her choices.

When Mrs. Hale stepped away from him after gently embracing him and welcoming him home, Jessica went to him and did the same.

* * *

Sitting beside her husband in Pastor Corelli's den, Raylene Finch couldn't help looking across the room at Vern Tompkins. The man Pastor Corelli and Pastor Hale had been on their way to see when the accident had happened. Rose had told Raylene that they'd been heading over to his place to pray with him to receive Christ. Rose had also told her that she and Stephanie Hale had prayed with him instead. At the hospital the day after the accident.

Raylene looked closely at the big man. He had spent decades without the knowledge of Christ's love for him. His entire life until a couple weeks ago. Lost. When she considered the unlikely friendship of her pastor and poor Pastor Hale, a friendship that had obviously compelled Mr. Tompkins, a friendship based on the power and simplicity of the gospel both men believed and indifferent to all the things beyond that which would have divided most people, Raylene began to wonder how many people there were in the world who would remain lost because of Christians being too busy fighting and debating and disagreeing and writing apologetics among themselves to notice them. When they all arrived in Heaven safe and sound, would God show them the lost people they had overlooked in their righteous rush to enlighten some brother or sister in Christ about his or her error in doctrine or thinking? She suspected He would. She wondered if He'd allow the eternally doomed lost a moment to look in the eyes of the Christians who had been all around them. Surely they'd have words to say if so.

You mean you knew all along how I could have been saved from an eternity apart from God and you never told me?

You had time to talk about football with me. You had time to complain about the weather to me. You had time to tell me that so-and-so from such-and-such church was a kook. Why didn't you have time to tell me I could be saved?

Thanks a lot. Some friend you turned out to be.

Raylene knew that they'd all know fully when they got to Heaven and saw Christ face to face. She suspected that she'd find out she'd been wrong about a doctrinal issue or two herself and that that *kook* from the church down the street had been right about this or that after all. Raylene figured she could deal with that knowledge. She'd have plenty of time in Heaven to apologize to any Christian she had considered *kooky* on earth and to accept their apologies for considering her *dead in the Spirit* or whatever else they'd thought of her.

But she did not think she could handle seeing the faces of people she'd failed to reach out to with the message of salvation in Jesus. Especially anyone she might have been speaking to during the times she'd chosen instead to complain to someone about her pastor or laugh with someone about some TV preacher she'd seen or to outright slam a different church.

She could console herself to a point with the knowledge that God pursued lost people. If Raylene failed to speak with them for whatever reason, God would surely lay it upon another believer's heart.

Right?

And maybe eventually, one of those believers would speak to that person and they'd get saved after all, even if a little later than they might have.

But Raylene was no idiot.

People died every day, many of them having never heard the gospel of Christ, or only having seen the splintered and often obnoxious representation of Him that was currently being put forth by His church as a whole. Oh, there were good people, millions of them, in good churches that did good things. No doubt about it.

But the picture as a whole?

It was nothing Raylene Finch wanted to think too long or hard about. At least not yet. Not on the day when she was welcoming her pastor home after he'd nearly lost his life.

A pastor Raylene would be calling on soon. Maybe after a couple days. After the Christmas Eve service. After he'd had a little more time to recuperate physically and to adjust to the fact that he'd sooner or later have to adjust to the fact of Pastor Hale's death.

Raylene owed him an apology.

* * *

The elevator doors slid open in front of him and Kent Sherman stepped out into the hospital's main lobby.

He'd just missed Pastor Corelli, the nurse at the desk upstairs had told him. He'd gone home just an hour before.

Kent had been to the hospital several times since the accident. He'd looked in on Pastor Corelli when he knew that nobody who would recognize him was around. But he hadn't spoken to the man even after he'd learned he'd regained consciousness.

That's what he'd intended to do today. Speak to the man. He'd labored over the decision all morning only to arrive at the hospital to find Pastor Corelli gone.

That was always the way it went with Kent. Just missing things. Appointments. Opportunities. The right woman.

He sighed and zipped his coat up for the trek across the parking lot to his car.

He'd missed figuring out what was going on with and inside Molly Avery until it was too late to use that knowledge to his advantage. He'd missed out on enjoying the fact that she had agreed to move in with him because she'd done so after those two pastors had put the hope of inner peace and purpose out in front of him at Thanksgiving dinner.

It was that hope that had brought Kent to the hospital. And it was the embracing of that hope that Kent Sherman did not want to miss.

Days ago, he had asked Molly Avery to move out and she had. Their relationship was over. Whether this Jesus stuff was true or not, Molly was not the right woman for Kent. If the things those pastors had said about Jesus were true, then Molly Avery had trampled all over Him for Kent, and that sickened him. Not only that, if the things those pastors had said about Jesus were true, Molly, if she really loved him, should have been way more concerned about his eternal soul than about her own pathetic need to hang on to her relationship with him no matter the cost. And if the things those pastors had said were not true, then Molly Avery was the worst kind of miserable and Kent wanted nothing to do with that.

Could it be that Molly's Jesus really did exist? Could it be that He would extend grace, unmerited favor as Pastor Hale had explained it, toward Kent? Even after Kent had sinned himself and had helped Molly Avery to sin?

As he drove, he realized that it would require unmerited favor from God for anyone, even good people, to really be found clean in His sight. That's why people used the word *saved*. If people could attain to their own perfection somehow, then God wouldn't need to give grace. He wouldn't have needed to die on the cross. He really wouldn't even have needed to be born as a man.

Kent squeezed his eyes shut for a second and them quickly opened them again. This stuff was mind boggling.

But there was one thing he did understand. If God was real, and if He did want to extend grace, unmerited favor, to him, Kent Sherman did not want to miss it.

He pulled his car into his slot in his apartment complex's parking lot and reached to kill the engine. But as his hand touched the cold metal base of the key, he thought once again about Thanksgiving dinner. It had been at Pastor Corelli's house. Kent was sure he could find it again.

No, he told himself.

The man had just gotten out of the hospital. He had lost his friend. He'd have family all around, people calling on the phone, two weeks of paper-work waiting for his attention.

He wouldn't have time to talk to Kent. And he probably wouldn't even want to. Kent knew because he'd overheard several of Molly's telephone conversations with some of the other women from her church, that Pastor Corelli had endured a lot of bickering and grief over his refusal to marry Molly to him. Kent Sherman was undoubtedly not one of Paul Corelli's favorite people.

That's why he'd been intending at first to speak with Pastor Hale.

But that was before the accident.

Kent shifted his car into reverse and backed out of the slot he'd just pulled into.

He had to try to talk with Pastor Corelli. He had to have his questions answered and the tugging, the prodding, the need he'd begun to sense with every conscious thought addressed. And he felt strangely confident that Pastor Corelli wouldn't mind helping him.

Kent realized even as he shook his head at the crazy irony of it, that the reason he could know that as surely as he did was that Pastor Corelli had already proven, with his refusal to officiate the wedding of all things, his commitment to Kent's proper understanding of faith in God and therefore ultimately to his eternal well-being.

His eternal well-being.

That was what he didn't want to miss.

* * *

His light was turned off, his shade pulled nearly down to the floor, and his room still wasn't dark enough to suit him.

Darkness.

That's what he felt.

That's what he deserved.

That's what he was.

Zeke Hudson moved from his chair down to the floor where the heat vent had just started blowing out warm air.

He was cold too.

All the time cold.

He had tried to do right by his father. At first by avenging his suicide by punishing churches because his father's church had devoured and destroyed him after his sin and repentance. Then he'd tried to do right by his father by thinking about getting his own life right with God again by responding to God's persistent beckoning in his mind's quiet and in somehow putting those words in Jon Hale's mouth that night at the coffeehouse.

You can't outrun Him and He's not going away.

Zeke had heard those words…and he had run. Not only that, he'd burned Jon's father's church. For no other reason than because he was furious that God would put words on Jon Hale's tongue to comfort and draw him back but hadn't sent anyone with words on the tongue to tell his father's church to forgive him. So he'd kept running. Trying to outrun God.

But he couldn't.

The trouble was, he couldn't turn back either. He

didn't trust God to take care of him. God hadn't taken care of his father, and his father had loved Him. At least in the beginning. Until he began to cheat. On his wife. On his calling. On his God.

Zeke knew that God would have forgiven him when he repented, and he wondered how all of their lives might have been different if anyone in the church would have done the same.

His mother had forgiven him, but she'd never been able to forgive the church for his suicide afterwards. She spent most of her time in the living room smoking cigarettes and watching TV preachers.

Running from God too, Zeke figured, like him. Except that she thought she wasn't since she was still exposing herself to His Word and to teaching.

Still, Zeke had tried to turn back. To be around Christians. To go to church. To realize that God might have tried to intervene on his father's behalf only to be ignored. By the church, and even by Zeke's father.

After all, God would not have led his father to kill himself. And God would not have led the church in unforgiveness.

And when it came right down to it, God would not have led his father into adultery, which had been the beginning of all of it.

None of it was God's fault. It was all sin. All of it. Ignoring God. Doing the wrong things.

But Zeke knew that if he stopped being angry at God, stopped blaming Him, he'd have to be angry at his father. Blame his father.

He couldn't do that.

And it wasn't enough to just blame the self-righteous loud-mouths of his father's congregation.

Zeke had begun to think he might actually be able to make it all the way back to God. He'd have to admit that he'd been running. He figured he could do that. He'd have to confess that he and his group of friends had been vandalizing all the churches in town. He figured he could do that too. He'd have to tell Pastor Hale that it had been him who'd burned his church. He figured he could even do that, though it wouldn't be easy.

But then Jon Hale had made that comment at the coffeehouse. The one about people not coming to the Christmas Eve service.

Who cares?

And the look in his eye and his self-righteous loud-mouthed tone had been too close to that of the people in his father's church, and Zeke had gotten angry.

Really angry.

So he'd messed with Jon's car. He still had the cross wrench he'd used here in the very room where he was sitting in the dark. The wrench he'd found in the toolbox in the back of the Hale's 4x4.

He'd figured Jon would get the vibration on his way home. Have to stop and walk or something. Get a little chilly. Suffer a little. He didn't expect anyone to drive the vehicle fast. Or on the Interstate.

He didn't expect anyone to die.

And Pastor Hale…

Darkness.

That's what Zeke Hudson had become.

God would never take him back now. Never.

And even though he deserved unforgiveness, it made him angry.

If only the Christians in his father's church had forgiven his father. None of this would have happened. He'd still be a rebellious pastor's kid. His mother would still be singing worship songs. His father would still be alive. He wouldn't have committed any crimes.

Vandalism. Arson.

Zeke pressed the heels of his hands hard against his eyes and it still refused to be dark enough.

Murder.

If only those people had forgiven his father. They were Christians, weren't they? Zeke knew they were because his father had preached to them and his father had been a great preacher.

He wondered how many of those unforgiving Christians were planning to attend the Christmas Eve service. He wondered how they'd feel if someone came along and shattered their worlds the way they had shattered his.

He could make it happen. He knew of a way.

And he had absolutely nothing to lose anymore.

"I'm going to do right by you, Dad," he whispered to his dark room. Then he got to his feet.

He had work to do.

20

Will Cooper leaned against the living room wall and waited for his father to say something. It was Christmas Eve day and they had just rearranged their living room furniture. At his father's insistence.

"It's time to move forward," he had said.

So the two of them had moved tables, chairs, lamps, the sofa, the entertainment center, and even the artwork hanging on the walls. Will had watched as his father placed some of the artwork and a couple of decidedly feminine table accents into a box, and as he'd put a stack of his four-wheel-drive magazines on top of the coffee table. He'd stacked them neatly at first, perfectly, but then he'd told Will to "mess them up a little" and Will had.

Will wasn't sure what to think of the new arrangement. He had never seen the house looking any other way than it had each day since the day of his mother's death until now.

"So what do you think?" his father wanted to know.

"It's...different," was all Will could say honestly.

"Yup," his father said. Then he crossed the room to stand right beside Will with his back against the wall too. "It's a start, anyway."

"We can always put it back."

His father breathed out long through a strained expression. "No, Will. It's you and me now and we've got to make our own home."

Will nodded.

He figured he could get used to the new room, and he knew he'd have no trouble getting used to not having to keep things so forced and predictable and perfect.

Maybe he and his father could even eat in the living room once in a while.

But Will had no intention of pushing his father in that or any other direction. He was content to enjoy the progress, the surprises, as they occurred.

Like the Christmas gifts sitting on the kitchen counter. This was a first too, and Will felt like a kid, so excited to see what his father had chosen for him that he could hardly wait to get his hands on the boxes.

But he would wait.

"I'm going to start counseling with Pastor Corelli right after the first of the year," his father said beside him. "I'm not sure how it's going to go. I trusted Alec. Respected him."

Again Will nodded.

"Corelli," his father said, "I really don't even know him."

"He's done counseling for years and years too, sir," Will said, even though he knew his father already knew that and even though he knew it hadn't been Pastor Hale's experience in counseling that had earned his father's trust or respect.

Pastor Hale had basically single-handedly turned things around for Will and his father. He had been there when they'd needed him. He had directed them toward God. He had prayed with and for each of them.

And he would have baptized them both in water.

Pastor Corelli could perform the baptism, Will knew, and he and his father had already decided together to ask him to.

But it wouldn't be the same.

"Do you suppose the whole church will just join Pastor Corelli's church now?" his father wanted to know.

"I don't think so," Will said. "They believe differently about a lot of stuff. I don't really understand all of it, but some of it is major." Will looked down at his feet. "Jon says Mr. Quinn is going to start pastoring the church once the building is finished."

His father stayed quiet for several long moments before he said, "It won't be the same." Then he pushed himself away from the wall, scanned the changed room one more time, and turned, rubbing his hands together, to face Will. "So what do you say we open our gifts before we head out for the service?"

Will smiled. "Really?"

"Sure."

Will followed his father through the living room and into the kitchen. A real Christmas. In every sense of the word. He and his father were together. Home. They had gifts to exchange. They'd go to church...to the biggest church service this town had ever held. And they both understood, really understood, for the first time in either of their lives the true reasons why Christmas was something to celebrate.

So even though there hadn't been a whole lot to celebrate during the days since Pastor Hale's death, Will Cooper allowed his mind to forget, for these few moments, everything but his thankfulness to God.

A real Christmas.

* * *

Jenna Lachlan arrived at the arena several hours before the Christmas Eve service was scheduled to begin. She wanted to position her camera people, but more than that she hoped to find a quiet place to sit for a while and attempt to sort and file all the conflicting emotions clamoring for her attention. Anticipation. Dread. Appreciation. Disgust. Thankfulness. Cynicism. Hope. Skepticism.

The quiet place to sit portion of her plan was not meant to be. The sound system guys were running sound checks. The musicians were tuning their instruments and practicing some of the Christmas carols and hymns they'd be leading the crowd in. Jenna couldn't help feeling a certain amount of amusement over the idea of people who normally used bass guitars in their worship services playing hymns. *Who sings hymns anymore, anyway? It's not possible to jam to 'Crown Him With Many Crowns' is it?* Those musicians had certainly had to swallow some pride for the sake of this Christmas Eve service. But Jenna had no doubt that there had been some serious pride-swallowing going on among the musicians from the other churches too. Churches where they only sang hymns and only used an organ or a piano. *A bass guitar and 'Crown Him With Many Crowns' occupying the same stage at the same moment? Guitars are tools of Satan, aren't they?*

Many different adjectives for how this service could turn out had entered Jenna's mind at one point or other since she'd first begun covering it and especially since the 'accident' that had killed Pastor Hale, but the only one she felt confident of at this point was *interesting*. One way or the other, no matter what happened, it would definitely be *interesting*. And since this was the first time in years that anything having to do with God or church or religion had earned that adjective in Jenna's mind, she was determined to not miss a minute of it. To not miss anything.

Deep down inside, even though she had no love for Christianity anymore and even though a disaster would make a better news story, Jenna hoped that the service would be a success. She hoped that all the different musicians from all the different churches could play the same songs without making nasty faces at one another. She hoped that none of the pastors who had been asked to speak would spend any of their allotted time criticizing one another. She hoped that the pentecostals wouldn't raise their hands while they were singing and she hoped that the Baptists wouldn't point at them and laugh if they did. She hoped that Satan—if he was real—would be too scared to assign his demons—if they were real—to this place and that God—if He was real—would send His angels—if they were real—to guard it.

She hoped that the service would honor the dead pastor.

He deserved that much.

Jenna Lachlan found a place to sit and settled in for the long wait for the beginning of the service. She listened to the music. She watched the people. She jotted down some of her thoughts.

And she prayed.

God, it's been forever since I've thought about You. Somehow, though, I know You're watching now and I know that this, if it goes well, is something that'll make You happy. Please help everyone who asks You to and please help...those of us who don't.

Jenna opened her eyes and nervously glanced around to make sure nobody had seen her with her head bowed.

Then she had to laugh at herself.

As if anyone in this place would mind!

* * *

Lifting her forehead from the cool comforter, Stephanie Hale stood from where she'd been kneeling to pray, on the floor beside Alec's side of the bed, and straightened her skirt.

Her black skirt.

Elise had just called up the stairs to her. It was time to head over to the arena if they wanted to find Jon before the service and show him where they'd be sitting.

"I'll be right down, sweetie."

Stephanie crossed the room to her dresser and looked in the mirror to adjust her jewelry and her makeup and her hair. Everything seemed to require so much cold and mechanical effort. Like choosing the clothes she'd wear to the service. Nothing in the closet had looked any better or worse to Stephanie. They were all just clothes and nobody would care anyway.

Except somewhere inside herself, though she had to strain to find that place, Stephanie cared. She wanted to attend the service. In God's honor. In Alec's honor. She wanted to look her best. To be her best.

She wanted to show everyone in the place and the whole rest of the world that she couldn't be prouder of Alec's vision for this service. That she couldn't be prouder of being his wife. That she, through God's strength and grace in her, would not surrender anything to the enemy on account of Alec's death.

But she felt disconnected. Like she was only taking each next step out of sheer force of will.

She knew from experience that this was a normal part of grieving, so she tried not to be too hard on herself. But she didn't want to baby herself either.

God still deserved her love and service.

Her children still needed her. Now more than ever before.

She practiced smiling for a few moments in front of the cold silent mirror and then joined Elise downstairs.

"You look beautiful," she told her daughter. "And strong. Daddy would be proud of you."

Elise smiled as she reached into the entryway closet for their coats. "Don't you think he knows what's happening?"

Stephanie nodded.

"Then he *is* proud of me," Elise said. "Not would be."

"Yes." Stephanie pulled Elise close to her and hugged her. Clung to her, really. But she reigned in her weakness and her fear and her loneliness, and when she looked at her daughter again after letting go of her, she was smiling. For real. "And we're proud of him."

21

Mayor Tom Stockton sat beside his wife near one of the exits at the arena as seats filled up all around them. He was not a church going man. Never had been. He'd toyed with the idea of starting to attend somewhere when he'd first gotten into local politics. Voters liked to see footage of their representatives on the steps of churches. It was a fact. But Tom had decided against it. He'd grown up in this town and everyone who was anyone knew him. It would have been obvious, what he was up to by suddenly, miraculously, becoming a church man. It would have cost him more votes from the people who knew him than it could have earned him from strangers.

Besides, what people in this part of the country wanted to see more than anything else was footage of their representatives doing their jobs. And that's what Tom Stockton was doing here today. On Christmas Eve.

His job.

His office had been besieged during recent days by complaints about this service. More specifically, by complaints about what might happen if these people actually succeeded at pulling it off and ended up doing even more things together. The local tavern owners' association, the local homosexual rights activists, the local chapter of some doctors for the rights of women organization, the local casino owners, just to name a few, had been on the phones and in his office in person to ask him what he intended to do about it.

"Do you know what'll happen, Mayor, if all these right wing wackos actually put their minds and resources together? This town'll be thrown back to the dark ages, that's what."

Personally, Tom thought that all these religious people put together didn't have enough mind power or resources to orchestrate the construction of a bird-house let alone any kind of serious political protest or threat. He also thought that it was one thing to get together and sing Christmas carols but quite another thing to put too many shoulders to the same wheel without someone's toes getting stomped on. And he knew that even if they did manage it, they still had to live by the laws of the land and would therefore be limited in what they could realistically accomplish. At least as far as tavern business and homosexual rights and abortion and gambling were concerned.

"All the good things in life," one of the people who'd come to see him had called them.

Well, Tom wasn't so sure about that end of it, but

he was sure that nothing much could come of this Christmas Eve service. It was a warm and fuzzy touchy feely whenever it rains God'll make a rainbow kind of thing and nothing more.

Certainly nothing dangerous.

Still, he was surprised to see so few empty seats remaining half an hour before the program was to begin. And all the people still coming in.

"Good evening, Mayor," an older gentlemen said to him as he walked by. "Merry Christmas."

"Yes. Merry Christmas," Tom said. He didn't recognize the man who had spoken to him, but wasn't necessarily troubled by that. These were primarily church people. People he ordinarily preferred to keep at a comfortable distance. He'd let them do their thing as long as they left him alone to do his.

Oh, there had been a few confrontations during his term. Marches at the local abortion clinic. Things like that. But there were really only two or three churches in town that ventured into the crafty and shrewd waters of the sea of policy making. And they had never, to Tom's knowledge—which was considerable, joined forces.

It was a good thing too, he thought now.

The arena was full and people were still coming in. Lining up against the walls and in some of the aisles to stand through the service.

Who knew that there were this many Christians in town?

In his town.

Tom knew that many of the people in the arena

this Christmas Eve had driven in from other places because of the publicity the event had gotten from Ms. Lachlan, especially after that pastor's death.

Many of the people. But not most.

Tom leaned back in his chair and breathed out slowly through his nose as he folded his arms across his chest. "Lots of church people," he said to his wife.

"Just smile," she told him.

* * *

Vern Tompkins sat between the Corelli family and the Hale family, what was left of it, in the front row to the left side of the platform. Pastor Corelli was scheduled to close the service and these seats had been reserved for him. He felt a little like a baboon in a lamp store sitting among the program participants. Pastors and their wives and children. Christian educators. Christian business owners. A local Christian writer. All influential people in the faith he had just accepted. And who was he? He owned a tackle shop, for crying out loud. And he could count the number of days he'd belonged to their religion on his fingers without counting any of them twice. But Stephanie Hale had invited him to sit with her. And that meant a lot to him.

Vern stood when the guy on stage told everyone to and bowed his head when the guy said to and then said amen when everyone else did.

Two months earlier, Vern had been sitting in the café sipping coffee and thinking nothing about God. And now, here he was, in the front row of what was certainly the highest attended church service in the history of the town rubbing shoulders and saying amen with a bunch of preachers.

Whoever had first said that the Lord works in mysterious ways had certainly known what he was talking about.

After the amen, the musicians went to the stage and the singing started. Some of the songs were familiar to Vern, but most weren't. They had the words projected onto a huge screen at the back of the platform, but that didn't help much. Vern attempted to keep up during the first couple of songs he didn't know, but eventually decided he'd get more out of them if he just read the words and listened.

Some of the music was soft and reverent sounding. The way the music always was during funeral scenes in movies. Some of the music was loud and thumpy, like the music in all the new commercials aimed at kids. And some of the music was the kind that Vern liked. Acoustic. Lots of tight harmony. A good but not overpowering beat. Nice clear words.

That's what Vern liked best about this music.

The words.

Stand up and sing
To God the King
Lift up your voice
Make a joyful noise
Come on, clap your hands
To the Great I Am
Lift up your voice
Make a joyful noise

Let's celebrate
His love is great
His hand is mighty
Mighty to save
So give Him praise
Now and always
Now and forever
Our God reigns

God's hand was indeed mighty to save. Vern Tompkins was proof of it.

* * *

Mighty to save?
Not in Zeke Hudson's world.
Nope. God hadn't done any saving there.
But Zeke clapped his hands and sang. He'd gotten a seat right where he'd wanted to. On the floor a few rows back from the platform. He was overly warm in the crowd and in his father's huge wool hunting coat, but he clapped his hands and sang. He had a headache the size of Mrs. Woodrow's 7th grade band class and a stomachache to pound right along with it, but he clapped his hands and sang. And he even managed a smile or two for the strangers on either side of him.

He hoped that the singing would get over soon and that whoever stepped onto the platform afterwards wouldn't ask the audience to take a few moments to greet the people around them. His father had done that during his church services. One song's worth of time to shake hands, smile, say praise God, smile some more, hug, and smile some more. Zeke had no intention of participating in that kind of nonsense tonight, and would lean forward in a fake fit of coughing if anyone approached him with more than a friendly nod.

Mercifully, the man who'd apparently be doing all the introducing of the evening got right down to business as soon as the musicians left the platform.

He spoke for a few moments in welcome, told the audience a little about what they could expect during the course of the evening. That was a waste of time if ever Zeke had seen one. They'd all been given programs and could see for themselves what they could expect during the course of the evening.

Zeke had to smile, though. Tonight's audience would be getting something that was not printed on their pretty little Christmas green programs.

Something big.

The smile was snatched away from him by the image that appeared on the giant screen behind the small man at the podium.

A photograph of Pastor Hale.

As the guy at the podium spoke about Pastor Hale's dream to have this service and about the tragic death he had died and then as the image on the screen disappeared and the small man introduced Mrs. Hale, Jon, and Elise, sweat piled up on Zeke's upper lip and around the back of his neck. It clung to him even as the Hales returned to their seats and the small man started in on another introduction.

Zeke hadn't anticipated the giant photograph of

Pastor Hale, and supposing that he probably should have did little to ease his sudden inability to pull in a decent breath.

Another little man stood in front of the huge white screen.

Zeke paced his breathing and uncurled his tight fingers.

He had to keep calm.

Until exactly the right moment.

* * *

For the first time in his ministry, Pastor Byron Smith felt ill at ease behind the pulpit. He had, of course, as every preacher did, dreamed of finding himself in the middle of the opportunity to speak to a gathering as large as this. His scripture text, which had been assigned to him by Pastor Paul Corelli, was compelling enough, and given the makeup of the audience, safe enough. He'd prepared what he thought was a relevant and stirring discussion of it. And he knew that the Lord would receive honor from the service as a whole.

And yet he felt nervous.

Not quite competent enough.

Not deserving enough.

It had been years since he'd gone to the pulpit in this type of humility, he realized to his own shame. Years. Not that he'd allowed himself to become arrogant or boastful, though he knew that other clergy often referred to him in those terms. He'd simply become confident in his preaching ability. In his ability to sense the Holy Spirit. In the safeness of his own pulpit.

Now he stood at an unfamiliar pulpit in a huge facility among other equally or more competent leaders…and he felt unworthy.

So he asked God to help him.

And God did.

* * *

Pastor after pastor, four men and one woman went to the pulpit and elaborated on their pre-selected passages of scripture until the whole Christmas story had been told and every believer in the place had been challenged to more closely repre-sent the love of Christ, a love that had led Him to the manger and then to the cross, to the lost and unsaved people around them.

"Look around you," the man now at the pulpit, Pastor Terry Stoltz, urged each person present. "Think of the army we could be. All of us here in one place…it kind of makes you wonder, doesn't it? How many of you could lift your hand and say that you knew there were this many Christians in your town?"

Even though a spotlight shone directly at him and he couldn't see whether people were or were not lifting their hands, he paused for half a second to allow his point to settle. "I realize we have many visitors from out of town here, but even if only half of us are local Christians…just think of what we could accomplish as Christ's one church."

Terry knew that he was treading on slippery

ground. If the men on his board were representative of an overall sentiment that it was sinful to work with people who didn't agree with you about the significance of the ninth toe of the beast, then he'd be wasting his breath. And he might be risking his pastorate besides. His board's annual vote to keep him on or not was coming up at the first of the new year.

But he didn't care.

When he'd seen all these people together in this one place standing as one in celebration of the Savior Who united them—even if they were too distracted to realize it—he'd had to say something.

"I know we don't see eye to eye on everything," he said. He allowed only a moment of the crowd's nervous laughter. "And don't get me wrong, doctrine is important. It determines how we live and how we understand God. It determines many of the stands we take. We are called upon in scripture to study to show ourselves approved. So doctrine is important and we should study it and we should know why we believe what we believe and be able to tell anyone who asks." He paused again. No nervous laughter from the crowd this time. "But, when we are standing at the Judgment when God separates those who knew Him from those who did not, I doubt any doctrine is going to seem as important as that of salvation by grace. A doctrine all of us share. The doctrine that can save the lost. The only doctrine, when it comes right down to it, that's going to put more people in the 'those who know Him' category at the Judgment."

Terry thanked the crowd for listening to him and

stepped away from the pulpit. As he passed Pastor Corelli on his way down from the platform, the man nodded at him and gave him an outright sign of strong and appreciative approval.

The old thumbs-up.

Terry decided that he'd call Pastor Corelli if his board decided not to vote him out after tonight's comments.

Maybe Pastor Corelli would still be interested in praying with Terry even though it had taken him all these months and a flat-out wake-up call from God to realize what a great idea it was.

Terry hoped so.

Then, suddenly, he wondered if as many people would have attended this service if Alec Hale had still been alive to participate in it.

Probably not.

The out of town people definitely wouldn't have come. They'd come to support a murdered pastor's vision. They'd come to stand with the local Christians against the hate that had motivated the vandalism and burning of churches and may have instigated Alec Hale's accident and death on the Interstate. Certainly, though, they could have celebrated Christmas Eve at home.

Persecution had brought them here. And it had probably brought many of the local people as well.

To stand against a common enemy.

Maybe persecution was the only thing that would shake comfortable and set-in-their-ways churches out of their divisiveness.

Terry hoped not.

But if so, and if the end of The Book happened any way close to the way Terry figured it would, Christians would soon be forced to overlook things like the proper length for a woman's skirt or a man's hair, whether one should use wine or grape juice during the observance of the Lord's Supper, what day to call the Lord's day, and even the more weightier things like which interpretation of the Bible was the most authentic, whether or not to believe that God still heals through the laying on of hands, and in Whose name people are baptized and at what point in their lives. They'd have to unite to stay alive. They'd have to unite in order to have any impact on an increasingly troubled and stubborn world.

Maybe people like Pastor Hale and Pastor Corelli were misunderstood because they'd inadvertently stepped out ahead of the inevitable timetable.

But Terry had to wonder, given the way Pastor Hale had died, if maybe the rest of them were just lagging behind it.

Terry stopped halfway down the steps and turned back toward the podium. "Can I say one more thing?" he asked Pastor Corelli.

Pastor Corelli nodded and the man who'd gone to the podium after Terry stepped aside to surrender the microphone back to him.

"Right now we're here to celebrate our Savior's birth," he said, grateful that the other pastor had chosen to stand beside him rather than returning to his seat. "We're also here, in a very real way, to stand as one against the kind of hatred that turned someone or many someones in our town into vandals, arsonists, and possibly even murderers."

Terry leaned closer in to the microphone. "I think that we, as one, need to pray for the person or persons responsible for these things. I think we need to pray that they will come to the knowledge of God's love for them and seek His forgiveness. And," he concluded, struggling with his voice because it seemed to want to abandon him, "I think we need to be willing to offer them our forgiveness. As one."

He thought of the Hale family, seated in the front row.

"A few of us have more to forgive than the rest of us. A lot more. But where would any of us be if Christ had been unwilling to forgive us? And not only us. He even asked for the forgiveness of the men who had nailed Him to the cross."

* * *

Rose Corelli watched her husband walk stiffly to the pulpit and stand silently behind it. There had been a lengthy applause when Paul had been introduced, and Rose had thought that he was only waiting politely for it to end before starting to speak. The concluding comments of the service.

The applause had ended. The arena, with its more than five thousand people, was silent. And still, Paul's Bible, and his mouth, remained closed.

Bowing her head, Rose mouthed a silent prayer for him. She suspected that this might all be happening too quickly for him. He'd only learned of Alec's death a few days ago. Alec's picture on the screen had gotten to Paul. So had Pastor Smith's comments. And Pastor Stoltz's.

Now, standing in front of this large group of people with his arm in a cast and the side of his head still bandaged, Paul looked tired and vulnerable.

"I had stuff to say," he said after a moment that had seemed like a thousand, "but I'm just going to close by reading our final passage of scripture for the evening."

He opened his Bible and turned slightly to wait for the words to his text to appear on the huge screen behind him as they had been all night behind each pastor who had spoken.

In that one instant of waiting, a voice from the crowd behind her called out that *he* had something to say. Rose looked behind her first, but quickly redirected her attention back to her husband.

He had turned toward the people again and was instructing the technicians to hold off on the scripture for a moment. "All right then," he said to the guy who'd interrupted him, "come up and say it."

Rose watched in confused uncertainty as a young man in a coat that was too big for him walked straight and quickly to the platform and climbed up onto it to stand right beside Paul.

"That's Zeke Hudson," Justin whispered in Rose's ear, as if he thought she'd recognize the name.

She didn't.

But she recognized a person in turmoil when she saw one, and this Zeke Hudson looked ready to shatter.

Slowly, he pulled open his coat, reached inside,

and slowly lifted out a gun. The whole arena tensed in one unison audible gasp.

It was a big gun.

One of those semi-automatic things.

Rose fought the urge to scream.

Until she realized that Zeke Hudson had dropped the gun to the floor at Paul's feet.

"I broke in your church windows," he said almost too quietly for the microphone to pick up his words. But it did pick them up. "I spray painted your buildings and your sidewalks and your signs. I burned down Pastor Hale's church."

"Zeke," Jon Hale said, suddenly standing even as Vern Tompkins tried to keep him seated. "You burned Dad's church?"

"Yes," Zeke said, and Rose thought she could see tears in his eyes. "And, Jon," he said, "It…it was me who messed with your dad's car. It was me. I…I hated the church because they didn't forgive my dad after he sinned. He was their pastor, and he repented, and they wouldn't forgive him. He couldn't handle it and he killed himself. Those people stole my father from me and I never meant to…to…I never meant to kill…"

"Zeke," Jon Hale said, "I…I forgive you."

And then, from somewhere behind Rose, a man's voice, "I forgive you too."

Somehow Rose recognized his voice. Pastor Smith.

"So do I," said another man. Rose did not recognize his voice. But it didn't matter. He was one of the pastors whose church had been vandalized.

One by one, pastors, from places all over the arena, stood to tell Zeke Hudson the same thing.

They forgave him.

* * *

Jon Hale looked from Zeke to Pastor Corelli. He didn't know what would happen next. He really didn't even know why he had said what he'd said except that he'd known he had to say it.

And to do it.

The sound of a siren pushed its way into his awareness. So did the sound of his mother sobbing. His sister.

But Jon couldn't move.

Zeke began to tremble as he looked toward his gun on the floor.

Pastor Corelli moved quickly to grab it and hand it to one of the uniformed and armed police officers who had just mounted the steps to the platform three at a time.

"I came here to kill as many of you as I could," Jon could hear Zeke saying even as he was being led off of the platform, up the nearest aisle, and out of the building, "and then that guy prayed for my forgiveness. I never meant to…"

Jon sat heavily in his seat again and pulled his mother close to him.

He knew that in the days to come he'd have to fight to find sense and peace. He knew that he could blame himself. Zeke had been angry at him, not at his father. He could blame and hate Zeke—except he'd already offered Zeke his forgiveness. And he'd meant it.

Before God, he'd meant it.

Because look where unforgiveness—unforgiveness of unforgiveness—had gotten Zeke.

A stunned silence settled over the whole place, but after a while, Jon wasn't sure how long, Pastor Corelli asked the technicians to put his scripture on the screen and then he left the platform.

Jon had no idea how many bullets Zeke's gun could conceivably have held or how many people would have been injured or killed if Zeke had decided to empty it. He had no idea what would happen to Zeke now, and for one tense moment he couldn't even be sure that he really cared.

But he was sure of one thing.

God's sovereignty.

And he knew that nobody who had been in this arena on this night would ever be the same again.

They had seen what hate had—and might almost have—done.

And they had seen what Christian love could do.

Jon held tightly to his mother and closed his eyes.

They were burning.

Then he smiled slightly, wondering what his father would have thought about the way the Christmas Eve service had turned out.

When he opened his eyes again, Jon was staring directly at the empty platform and at Pastor Corelli's final scripture text silently but boldly waiting on the huge white screen.

"Now I am coming to You, and I speak these things in the world so that they may have My joy completed in them. I have given them Your word. The world hated them because they are not of the world, as I am not of the world. I am not praying that You take them out of the world but that You protect them from the evil one. They are not of the world, as I am not of the world. Sanctify them by the truth; Your word is truth. As You sent Me into the world, I also have sent them into the world. I sanctify Myself for them, so they also may be sanctified by the truth. I pray not only for these, but also for those who believe in Me through their message. May they all be one, as You, Father, are in Me and I am in You. May they also be one in Us, so the world may believe You sent Me. I have given them the glory You have given Me. May they be one as We are one. I am in them and You are in Me. May they be made completely one, so the world may know You have sent Me and have loved them as You have loved Me."
Christ Jesus—John 17:13-23

The End

CPSIA information can be obtained at www.ICGtesting.com
Printed in the USA
BVOW010407220911

271795BV00001B/1/A

9 781597 812009